FENELLA J MILLER

Hannah's War

Hannah's War Copyright Fenella J. Miller, 2012

This book is a work of fiction. While references may be made
to actual places or events, the names, characters, incidents, and
locations within are from the author's imagination and are not a
resemblance to actual living or dead persons, businesses, or events.
Any similarity is coincidental.

ISBN: 9781481061681

PARK PUBLISHING, COLCHESTER, ESSEX UK

Acknowledgements & Thanks

My thanks to the Edward Taplow who gave up
an afternoon to show me his farm and drive
me around the area.

As always for Susan Rhodes

Cover design: Jane Dixon-Smith

Dedication

In memory of Jack Cross & Frank Rhodes
who served in the RAF in WW2

Chapter One

November 1941, Essex, England.

'Shut that bleeding door, you stupid girl. If the pigs get out again I'll get rid of you, bugger me if I won't.'

Hannah blinked back tears. Mr Boothroyd was right to be angry, he'd told her often enough to lock the door when she came out of the sty. She flung herself at the gap. The door banged shut and she slammed the bolt home accompanied by indignant squeals from the unfortunate porker she'd clouted on the snout. Never mind she was on her knees in pig-muck, the wretched animals were secure and she wouldn't be sent packing.

Using the wall to prise herself up she turned to apologise to her employer. The yard was empty. Once he'd been sure his precious pigs were safe he'd stomped off to the warmth of his kitchen where his poor wife would be waiting to serve him a massive breakfast.

Her gumboots squelched as she headed for the barn, with each footstep a disgusting smell wafted up. Thank God tonight was bath night, even five inches of water, in the old galvanised tin bath in front of the parlour fire, was better than nothing. It was her turn to go first, Betty and Ruby wouldn't be impressed when they saw her. The thought of her co-workers' disgust made the smell almost worthwhile.

She'd drawn the short straw this week - pigs and chickens - she preferred the milking parlour even if you did have to get up at the crack of dawn. For some reason cow-dung didn't smell half as bad as pig or chicken muck, maybe because the cows didn't eat meat. Heaven knows what went in to the pig swill, and the farmyard fowl picked up everything including the unmentionable bits dropped from a muck filled wheel-barrow.

By mid-morning she'd finished her chores and went to the cottage to make a much-needed mug of tea. Betty and Ruby would be in the parlour scrubbing down, they wouldn't finish until lunchtime but at least would have the afternoon free until milking. If she was honest, she liked to be alone. The other two thought she was *stuck up*, talked with a plum in her mouth, was *too posh* to be part of the Women's Land Army. Having a double-barrelled surname didn't help.

However unpleasant the two Londoners were at least she was safe at Pond Farm. She shuddered and pushed away the dark images; *he'd* never look for her in the depths of the Suffolk countryside. But she jumped every time she heard a raised voice or saw a large black car.

There was the familiar drone of returning airplanes. She stopped and gazed upwards, automatically counting the bombers as they flew overhead. Two squadrons went out last night— how many had survived the sortie? Her heart thudded painfully. Nineteen... she held her breath. Were there anymore? Surely five couldn't have been lost in one night?

These were Blenheims, so Betty said... or were they Beaufighters? Both belonged to Squadron 25F based at Debfield and were almost identical in shape.

Thank God! Four more planes passed - only one more to return. She swallowed the lump in her throat; this was a painful reminder that her twin, Giles, was missing. He'd bailed out somewhere over France, but whether he was a POW or with the Resistance, she'd no idea. He couldn't be dead. If she hadn't been so miserable then she'd never have agreed to … She was jerked back to reality by the stuttering of a plane in trouble.

She scrambled over the gate in to the meadow. She watched the final bomber stagger across the sky, black smoke billowing from one engine. This was so low she could see the pilot struggling with the joystick. Her hands clenched and she sent up a fervent prayer he would get his plane the last few miles and land safely.

On impulse she waved her arms and cheered the plane on its way. To her astonishment the pilot raised his hand as if acknowledging her encouragement. She stood watching the horizon for tell-tale smoke. Five minutes passed. He had landed safely; smiling she ran back to the farm and headed for the small, two up two down, cottage she shared.

She needed to use 'the bucket and chuck it' which served as their lavatory. She smelt so appalling she scarcely noticed the stench inside the lean-to. She hooked off her boots and turned them upside down to drain then lifted the latch and put her shoulder to the door. She fell in to the room and skidded to a halt when she saw the girls.

'Bleedin' 'ell, Baggie, you smell worse than them pigs.'

Ruby Smith sniggered and chipped in her two-penny-worth. 'Betty's right. You stink, Baggie, and you ain't having first bath. I'm not bleedin' well getting in your water, that's for sure.'

'What are you doing in here? Shouldn't you be cleaning the parlour?' Attack was always wisest with these two.

Betty answered. 'If you get the bath will you promise not to tell that old blighter we knocked off for a cuppa and a fag?'

Hannah was tempted to argue but it just wasn't worth it.

Four planes had failed to return to the nearby 'drome over the past two weeks—how could she get upset about something as trivial as sneaking out for a ciggie? 'Fine. Is there any tea left in the pot? I'm parched.'

Betty shrieked and pinched her nose. 'Take them bleedin' socks off, Baggie, for gawd's sake.'

Grinning, Hannah removed them and, holding them at arm's-length carried them in to the scullery where she dropped them in to a bucket of water. Quickly scrubbing herself more or less clean, she returned to the warmth of the tiny kitchen. To her surprise Ruby handed her a steaming mug without any of her usual snide comments.

'Thanks, did you hear the planes going over?'

Betty pushed her stringy blonde hair out of her eyes before answering. 'I reckon several of them poor buggers bought it last night. Small wonder the boys in blue enjoy a party when they get the chance.'

'No - they all came back. I expect we'll hear when we go to the dance at the village hall on Friday night.'

'You coming, Baggie? You never went to the last two with us.'

'I know, Ruby, I was too tired then, but I think I've toughened up these past weeks, I don't feel so exhausted all the time. Mr Boothroyd said we can all go once the animals are sorted, and now I've got a bicycle I can come with you.'

'They'll be glad to see another girl, they was queuing up to dance with us last time and I'm no oil painting.' Betty smiled. Hannah thought maybe she was becoming part of the gang at last.

'They'll have to be desperate to want to get within three feet of me. It's going to take more than a bath to get rid of the stink of pig.'

'I've got a bottle of bath salts; I reckon if you tip half of that in you'll smell all right.'

'That's really kind of you, Ruby, thank you.' Hannah took

the only available chair and collapsed. 'I used to do everyone's hair at school; would you like me to do yours on Friday?'

'Do you reckon you could put mine in one of them fancy rolls like what we saw in the paper?'

Hannah tipped her head to one side. 'I'm sure I can, Ruby, it's more than long enough.' Replacing her mug on the table she pushed herself upright. 'I'd better go and find myself a pair of dry socks then get back to work. It's my turn to cook; I've got enough cracked eggs to make an omelette and pancakes to follow.'

*

'Thank God it's a full moon tonight, I was dreading having to cycle to the village hall,' Hannah said.

'After a couple of port and lemons you'll not notice the dark, Baggie,' Betty told her as she admired her own reflection. 'Ta ever so for doing my hair, I never knew it'd go up so nice.'

Hannah smiled. 'You both look jolly good and your bath salts worked wonders.' She pulled her jacket down over her hips and knotted her silk headscarf under her chin. 'Let's hope we arrive without mishap, it's more than two miles and the lane's full of potholes.'

Betty headed for the door. 'If we don't get a move on we'll be too bleedin' late for them boys in blue to buy us a few drinks before the dance starts. I ain't going across without a couple, they only serve tea in the hall.'

Hannah's bicycle had been discovered under a pile of junk at the back of the old barn. Fortunately the one remaining farm worker, Arthur, was a dab hand at repairing things and it looked splendid. Thank goodness no one seemed to bother with gas masks; this was one less thing to worry about.

Tonight was her first real outing on the bike, on the other occasions she'd been wearing dungarees not a frock with a swirling skirt. 'Betty, how do I keep my dress out of the wheels?'

A hoot of laughter greeted her question. 'Tuck it in yer knickers, ain't no one going to see you out here. We stop at the end of the lane to sort ourselves out and walk the last few yards.'

Balancing her cycle against one knee Hannah stuffed the hem of her dress in to her knickers; this was draughty but at least she would be safe. Her court shoes were in the basket at the front, along with her handbag. Like the other two her legs were bare; she'd drawn the seam down the back of each calf with an eyebrow pencil hoping this would make it appear she was wearing stockings.

'Righty ho! Keep them knees together tonight, Baggie, give them RAF blokes half a chance and you'll be on your back.'

Shocked to the core by Ruby's plain speaking Hannah wobbled violently and her front wheel clipped the gate. Before she could prevent herself she was in a tangle of pedals and wheels on the dirt.

'Bugger me, and we ain't even off the farm yet! Are you hurt, Baggie?' Ruby leant down and offered her hand.

'I'm fine, thank you. What a blessing I wasn't wearing stockings.'

Together they straightened the bike and examined it for damage. 'Looks sound enough, give it a push and see if it works.'

Obediently Hannah trotted a few paces and the bike rolled along smoothly. 'There, no harm done apart from the mud on my knees.'

'I reckon you'll have to nip in to the ladies' room at the pub and give yourself a clean-up. Now, can we get going?' Ruby swung nimbly on to her bike, her thighs gleaming in the moonlight. 'If you can manage to stay on board, Baggie, it'll be a bleedin' miracle.'

The ride to Debfield was punctuated by screeches from Betty and copious swearing from Ruby every time she bounced through a pothole. Hannah began to enjoy the experience and by the time they reached the end of the lane where they were to dismount she was convulsed with giggles. It had been too long since she'd had anything to laugh about.

Whilst she struggled to untuck her dress Betty and Ruby forged ahead bawling at her to hurry up. A group of RAF on cycles shot out from behind a hedge. Her bike crashed to the grass and her fingers scrabbled to restore her dignity.

Suddenly a broad back was in front of her blocking her from the view of the other two.

'Do you want any help, miss, Pete's a dab hand with knickers.'

Her knight in air force blue interrupted the raucous laughter. 'Shut it, you two, or I'll have you cleaning latrines for the next month.'

Her rescuer's companions vanished on their bikes. The last of her skirt dropped over her knees and she was decent. Thank goodness the man couldn't see her scarlet cheeks. 'Thank you for intervening—as you've probably guessed I'm new to this lark. I'm Hannah, by the way.'

He swung round. He was a head taller than her and *she* was overly tall for a female. He bent down and picked up the discarded bike with his left hand whilst balancing his own against his hip. 'Jack Rhodes, delighted to be of service to a damsel in distress.'

Her fingers disappeared in his; his grip was firm. She didn't like the contact and snatched her hand away. 'I take it you're an officer? Are you a squadron leader and those two your minions?'

'Flight Lieutenant, and those dimwits are my flight engineer and gunner. Do you have a surname or are you remaining anonymous?'

'Anonymous—can you imagine the furore if my family heard I'd been flashing my underwear at the RAF.' His deep chuckle made him seem less intimidating.

'In which case, I'll enquire no more. I take it you're going to the village hop? Are you coming to the pub first? I'd be delighted to buy you a drink to steady your nerves after your—your unfortunate encounter.'

Wheeling both bikes easily, he strolled beside her chatting as if they'd been friends for ever. He was charming, intelligent and a pilot - what more could a girl want in a dance partner?

The pub was all but invisible but the noise from the bar made it easy to find. 'I have to tidy myself before I can come in the bar, Jack. I fell off my bike at the farm and I'm covered in mud.'

'Did you hurt yourself? You could have several nasty cuts that need attending to. Joan's bound to have a first aid kit.' His voice was edged with concern. What a kind man he was; he'd only met her ten minutes ago and was treating her like a special friend.

'I pedalled all the way here with no difficulty. I'm rather accident prone so falling off a bike was nothing. Thank you for your help. Next time I'll be more adept at untucking my dress. Is there a side entrance I can use?'

He leant the bikes against a pile of others and handed over her bag and shoes; with his hand pressed in the small of her back he guided her around the building as if it was daytime. He must be a regular to know the layout so well.

'Here, nip in this way. The ladies' room is on your left, but the 'you-know-what' is down that path. Don't go there unless you have to.' His laugh was loud in the darkness. 'Don't be long will you?'

'I'll be as quick as I can.'

He rummaged in his pocket and pulled out a crumpled cotton square. 'Here, you might find this useful. It's perfectly clean. What would you like to drink? The beer here's pretty good.'

'A shandy would be lovely and thank you for the hand-kerchief. I won't be a jiffy.' She thought she'd handled the encounter pretty well, he couldn't possibly have known her hands were trembling, that she was nervous of being near a man.

The narrow corridor was dark, no one must allow the slightest glimmer of light to escape. The ARP wardens were vigilant close to any RAF bases. With her torch she spotted an oil lamp and a box of matches waiting on a bench inside the side door. Blinking in the brightness she turned to see the Ladies was right beside her.

There was a decent mirror, a bit brown in places, but good enough to give herself a quick wipe down. She tipped some water from the china jug in to the bowl. Her legs were grazed but nothing serious and the mud wasn't too bad. Jack's hanky was ideal and soon she was clean.

She dithered outside the door, her heart rapid, her hands clammy. She wasn't sure she was ready to face a crowd of strangers after being isolated on the farm these past weeks. But she would be safe in a crowd. The door swung open and a smiling woman greeted her.

'Come in, ducks, you must be Hannah; Jack has a nice glass of shandy waiting for you.' The speaker was in her forties, her curly brown hair liberally sprinkled with grey. 'I'm Joan Stock, landlady here. Pleased to meet you.'

She extended her hand and Hannah took it. 'Everyone's being so kind; I'm not used to … thank you.' It would be better not to dwell on her old life - things were different now. She'd never go back, even if *he* found her she'd refuse to leave. She was twenty-one on January 6th so just needed to be invisible until then.

Mrs Stock all but bundled her in to the crowded bar which was heaving with air force personnel plus a dozen or so girls about her age not in uniform. The smell of oil lamps and apple logs mingled with the cigarette smoke and the blue haze made breathing difficult. She froze waiting for heads to swivel, to be pinned by predatory male eyes. Being considered attractive was not something she enjoyed any more.

'Go on, ducks, they won't bite. Bleeding noisy lot, but harmless enough. Look, Jack's waving and Ruby and Betty are with him.'

No one stared at her, instead she was greeted by smiles and winks as she pushed her way through the tightly packed room. She wished the handsome pilot wasn't showing an interest, the very thought of him wanting to touch her made her stomach heave.

When she was within hailing distance Betty called out. 'There you are, Baggie, thought you'd done a runner. We've saved you a chair and Jack's got you a shandy.' There was little room around the small, wooden table. 'Budge up, Ruby; she'll not fit in otherwise, not with her long legs.'

Jack was draped over the window sill, her chair directly in front of him. He was too close. Waves of panic threatened to overwhelm her. She mustn't let what had happened spoil her life.

He grinned and held out a glass of frothing, brown liquid. 'I've got you mild and lemonade, I hope that's all right. If you'd prefer bitter, I can drink this and get you another one.'

'As I've never tasted either of them I've no idea which I prefer.' She squeezed past him and the buttons on his jacket dug in to her back. 'I don't drink much so I thought I'd start with something not too strong.'

Betty leant across the table to whisper loudly in her ear. 'Don't have too many of them or you'll be down the lav all night, and it's no fun in the dark, I can tell you. Goes right through you, a shandy does. Have a sweet sherry next time,

I should.'

Carefully Hannah raised a glass to her lips and took a small sip. It was surprisingly palatable, malty and sweet. She glanced at Jack. 'It's delicious, thank you. Will everyone be going to the dance?'

'Absolutely, we get tanked up and then stagger over. No alcohol served in the village hall and we try not to keep dashing backwards and forwards because of the blackout.'

Two airmen joined them and Betty and Ruby began to flirt outrageously. When the shorter of the two spoke she recognized him as the one who'd made the comment about knickers.

Embarrassed she turned away. Jack was looking at her with a stunned expression. 'Good God! You're the girl who waved the other morning; I've been racking my brains to think why you look familiar.'

Her mouth dropped open. 'I waited until I was sure you'd landed safely before I went in, I didn't expect to meet the pilot of *that* plane. What a coincidence.'

He bent down to speak to her, he would have to shout to make himself heard otherwise. 'Not really, we always come here when there's a dance. The White Hart's the only pub in the village with half decent beer. We were bound to meet eventually but I'm glad it was tonight.'

She was about to answer when the door burst open letting a flood of light out. An ARP warden shouted 'Everyone down the cellar, two German fighters heading this way.'

Chapter Two

The brimming shandy slopped on the table. Jack pressed Hannah in the chair. To his horror she stiffened and wrenched her shoulder away. His brow creased, she was as nervous as a kitten, he must take care or he'd frighten her away. She was new to this nonsense and didn't know nobody bothered with the cellar.

'Don't worry, Hannah, our chaps will be after them before they have time to do any damage. It's not bombers; if we stay away from the windows and doors there's no risk at all.' He crouched beside her. 'Jimmy's the ARP warden, he comes in but everybody ignores him.'

Her remarkable green eyes widened. 'Good heavens! Someone's giving him a pint of beer.' She tensed as the roar of half a dozen Spitfires shook the pub.

'This happens most weeks; the blighters follow us and attack just as we're coming in to land. They must have lost their way tonight.' She was straining back as if wanting as much distance between them as possible. He moved along the window-sill. She relaxed, but her smile was forced. If he had any sense he'd leave well alone, but something about her was drawing him in.

'Wasn't your airfield attacked earlier this year in broad daylight?' Her eyes glittered; she was definitely upset.

'Yes - and we lost a few planes and a lot of buildings, but things are better now, turning our way.'

Her friends were too busy nattering to Pete and Dave to notice he was monopolising her. He must be careful not to upset her again. When he'd first seen her his second engine was on the blink, the other one already stalled and he'd doubted he would get his crate down safely. Seeing the girl leaping up and down waving had been a good omen, somehow she'd become important to his crew's survival.

He was determined to involve her in his life. As long as she was, he'd return to base after each sortie. Even if she'd been as plain as a pikestaff he'd still have pursued her.

'My twin was shot down over France. I'm certain he's not dead, I'd know if he was. I'm praying he's with the resistance and will find his way home.'

'A lot of our bods bail out, and he'll not be that badly treated if he's captured, just have to remain incarcerated.'

She buried her face in her drink and when she looked back she was composed. 'When do we go to the village hall? Will there be a band or just records?'

'Neither, someone plays the joanna; he's really good, used to be with some big outfit before the war.'

Her smile did something strange to his insides. 'You didn't say when we're going? Presumably not until the all clear sounds?'

He glanced at his watch. 'Normally we decamp around seven o'clock; the locals have a sing-song. Not everyone comes for a pint first.'

'Good, only another twenty minutes. I can't remember the last time I danced, I've probably forgotten all the steps.'

The wail of the all clear was audible over the noise. With any luck the Spits would shoot the buggers down; he'd find out at the base later.

*

Hannah swung her chair round and made it part of the group. Jack was paying her too much attention, he was going to be disappointed if he expected her to respond. He was exactly the kind of chap who attracted girls; she'd have to be blind not to notice the envious glances of several young ladies.

Corn coloured hair and bright blue eyes were much better than dark hair and brown eyes. At least he looked nothing like … she couldn't even bear to say his name in her head. Angrily she pushed the memories away.

Ruby winked at her and leant forward to speak quietly in her ear. 'Bit of all right, your fellow. He can't keep his eyes off you. All the girls are after him I can tell you. Looks like one of them film stars, I reckon, and nice with it. Not a big head like some of the pilots.'

'I'm not interested, not in him or anyone else. I shouldn't have come; I should have stayed at home.'

'Blimey, Baggie, you've gone right pasty. You scared of men, or something?' Betty spoke softly so no one else heard.

'Something dreadful happened to me, I don't think I'll ever be able to trust a man again. Please don't tell anyone, I'm trying to forget about it.'

Betty squeezed her hand sympathetically. 'The bastard— some men need castrating like them pigs we do. Don't you worry about it; I'll see no one takes any liberties. No wonder you ran away. Good job you're not in the family way.'

Hannah couldn't believe she'd just blurted out her dark secret and to Betty of all people. The girl was shocked but didn't look at her in disgust, her face was full of sympathy. A weight began to lift from her shoulders

'The very thought of intimacy makes me sick. I'm not sure I'm going to be able to dance with Jack, I don't like the idea of him putting his hands on me.'

'Stop there, I'll fetch you a brandy. Get that down you

and you'll not think twice. I can promise you Jack won't hurt you, he's the gentlest bloke around.'

Hannah was relieved to see he was now talking to a couple of locals. She swallowed the brandy like medicine. The fiery liquid burnt a passage to her stomach and delicious warmth raced through her veins pushing her fears aside. For the first time in months life looked promising. Maybe she *was* ready to move on.

As soon as she'd drained her glass Betty winked and stood up. Hannah had never seen either of the girls out of their hideous uniforms. When they went out she always made herself scarce, found something to do in one of the barns until they'd gone and was asleep when they got back.

'Come along you two, I want to powder my nose before we go.'

Hannah hesitated, not wanting to push past a group of noisy airmen. A sharp dig in the back from Ruby reminded her they were supposed to be going to the ladies' room before the other girls had the same idea. There was already a queue to use the mirror to reapply lipstick and rouge and tuck in stray bits of hair.

A tall, thin girl with peroxide blonde hair gave her a friendly smile. 'About time; you must be Baggie, we've heard ever so much about you these past few weeks.' She extended her hand and

Hannah shook it. It seemed odd to be doing something formal when squashed in the ladies' room. 'Daphne Ranger, I'm on a farm at Wimbish with Pearl, the one with the *real* blonde hair, and Rita, who's had to go out the back.'

'Actually, my name's Hannah, I'd rather you called me that.'

'Fair enough. I reckon you're the prettiest here tonight— a real bit of class is what my ma would say.'

'It's my voice, I wish I spoke like everyone else. Thank you for the compliment, kind but totally untrue. I'm far too tall and flat-chested to be considered pretty.'

Ruby overheard this last remark and turned to join in the conversation. 'Stuff a couple of socks down yer front, no one will know the difference. It's what I do, and I've had no complaints so far.'

The shrieks of laughter following this remark made Hannah feel part of the group in spite of her crystal cut diction. Maybe if she added a few expletives, softened her vowels, she would be less obviously upper-class. If anyone from home came to Debfield they would find her easily, no one else around here looked or sounded like her.

She barely glanced in the mirror; she hadn't bought her makeup anyway. Someone doused the oil lamp and they trooped out the side door to be met by the flickering torches of the men waiting outside to escort them to the village hall.

'Betty, we don't have our overcoats and we'll need them to cycle back.'

'The dance only lasts a couple of hours; we go back for a nightcap and collect them. You worry too much, Hannah, let your hair down a bit, we work bleedin' hard and we're entitled to a bit of fun.' She moved closer and whispered. 'Don't look so worried, Ruby and I will keep an eye on you. Any beggar tries anything on and we'll flatten him.'

'Thank you, and thank you for calling me Hannah.'

In the crowd she couldn't identify individuals, the pin-pricks of light directed to the ground kept everyone's face in shadow. She stumbled; her feet didn't belong to her any more. She shouldn't have had the brandy. Jack's hand grasped her elbow but as soon as she was steady he released her.

'I'm surprised you don't spend most of your time in hospital, Hannah, I've never met another girl so accident prone.'

He was right; she would trip over a matchstick left in front of her without the added disadvantage of being slightly tipsy. 'Thank you, I can't tell you how much your encouragement means to me.' This wasn't what she'd intended to say, the last thing she wanted to do was flirt with him.

He was walking close enough for her to be able to smell a mixture of engine oil and carbolic soap, hardly an attractive aroma but somehow it made him less threatening, more like her and the other land girls.

'You're the perfect height for me. I'm sick of talking to the top of a girl's head when I dance. There's no one here tonight who's a patch on you. I saw you first so no-one else is going to get a look in.'

She felt as if a stone lodged in her stomach along with the double brandy. 'I'm not sure I'm going to be dancing at all, I don't really like …' How could she tell him she didn't want to be held without offending him?

'It's okay, we can sit on the stage and play brag if you like. No pressure from me, but you'd enjoy it, nothing like a bit of a knees-up to raise the spirits.'

Her fingers twisted her hair; she didn't know how to answer. He was right - dancing with him was what she needed. Tonight she would be like everyone else, just a girl enjoying a night out after working hard all week for the war effort. 'Very well, Flight Lieutenant Rhodes, I'll dance with you.'

His teeth flashed in the darkness. 'Jolly good! I'm beating them off with a stick most nights. I expect you've noticed I'm the most popular bloke around here.'

For a second she thought he was serious then she laughed. 'You must have difficulty putting on your cap, you've the biggest head of anyone for sure. Hurry up, everyone's gone and I'm freezing without a coat.'

He bustled her in then pushed aside the blackout. The room was bigger than she'd expected, at least fifty mismatched chairs against one wall and room on the other side for an upright piano and two long tables with the tea urn and cups and saucers. There were several small, deal tables on the stage occupied by villagers engrossed in card games. Someone had made an effort to make the place look festive with limp bunting and a single bunch of balloons.

The pianist was playing a melody of popular songs and the early arrivals were grouped around singing with more gusto than pitch. Everyone was smiling; it was hard to believe there was a war on. 'I wish I'd come to the last dance, I'd no idea I was missing such fun.'

'And I wish you'd come then I'd have known you a month and not an hour. Good show, the dancing's going to start. Next time we can come for the singing if you like.'

Her mouth curved. 'You're very sure of yourself - how do you know I won't be escorted by someone else?' She tilted her head and looked him up and down critically. 'I'm sure there must be a squadron leader or wing commander just dying to meet me.' His shout of laughter turned several heads; the alcohol had loosened her tongue, made her feel normal again.

'I'll introduce you if come to the base. Johnny Page, our squadron leader, is happily married with two small children. Gerard Stanton, the wing-co, has a tin leg as he lost the other one over Dunkirk.'

There was no time to tell him she might not get any more time off this month as the pianist launched in to a lively polka. She was swept off her feet as Jack twirled around the floor. She couldn't fault his enthusiasm but technique was sadly lacking. When they stopped her hair was coming out of its elaborate arrangement and perspiration beaded her forehead. But she'd loved every minute of it, not felt threatened or revolted by being so close to a man.

'Sorry about that, overdid it a bit, didn't I?' His engaging grin stifled her mild reprimand.

'It was great fun, but next time we dance I'd prefer my feet to be *on* the floor and not dangling in mid-air.'

'At least I didn't crunch your toes; I'm much better with

the waltz or quickstep.'

Her handbag was on a chair with Betty's and Ruby's. She needed a handkerchief to wipe her face before another rampage around the village hall. 'Excuse me, I must repair the damage.'

He nodded and turned to talk to Pete and Dave. If she danced with Jack again would he get the wrong idea? Was it better to be with someone she already trusted than be mauled by a perfect stranger?

'Cor, I'll be too knackered to cycle back if we have any more like that.'

'Betty, is Jack… is he … well you know, someone I should be careful of?'

'I *told* you, he's a real gent, never heard anyone complain about *him* taking liberties. There's half a dozen girls here wish he would. He'll not take advantage, can't say the same for some others here.'

'I'm reluctant to be close to anyone after what happened.'

'Then tell him you're engaged, he'll not pressure you then. Very respectful, everyone likes him and his crew think the world of him.'

The first notes of a waltz interrupted their conversation. There was a light tap on her shoulder and she tried not to pull away. He was standing behind her. 'Come along, don't stand gossiping all night, I want to show you I can waltz and make up for last time.'

The evening whirled past. By the time the last dance was over she'd forgotten her reservations, Jack was behaving like a brother, had kept his hands to himself and not made any improper suggestions. Betty and Ruby had left, in fact half the couples had drifted off. She shivered. Would Jack expect to kiss her when they were outside? She'd had no opportunity to tell him she was spoken for and wished she had.

Like most of the airmen he'd removed his jacket and

been dancing in his shirt sleeves. Instead of putting it on he draped it over her shoulders.

'It's going to feel damn cold outside; you'll need this until you get your overcoat from the pub.'

"Thank you, I've enjoyed this evening. I hope my legs aren't too rubbery to pedal back. We have to be up at dawn. I'm not going to stop for a nightcap.'

'If your friends stay then you must. You can't ride back on your own. God knows where you'll end up.'

'Cheek! Even I can manage to cycle in moonlight without falling off.'

He stood back allowing her to step in to the small, dark space between the front door and the blackout curtain. The pub door closed. He was too close. She was reaching out when he pulled her against him. 'No, don't…you mustn't … leave me alone.' In her panic her feet caught in the heavy material.

'Standstill, Hannah, let me sort this out. You'll have the whole thing down in a minute.' She could feel him fumbling about on the floor. She wanted to scream—didn't like being in the dark with him.

Suddenly the door behind them opened and they were catapulted forward. There was nothing she could do to save herself. With a horrendous crash the pole holding the curtain tore from the ceiling smothering them in choking darkness. Jack twisted his body to cushion her fall but her arm was trapped beneath them. A searing pain shot through it.

Her face was crushed against his shirt, his jacket slid down her arms adding to the confusion. She couldn't breathe. She struggled, increasing the agony in her arm. Then they were rolled over like a carpet to emerge, red-faced and gasping in front of the bar.

Her eyes were streaming, her hair straggling down her back and everyone was laughing.

'Up you come, miss, no harm done, I hope, apart from

to the blooming curtain and the ceiling.' Mrs Stock helped Hannah to her feet and brushed the worst of the dust and cobwebs from her dress.

'I'm so sorry, my feet caught in the curtain and then somebody sent us flying. I'll pay for any damage.' She swayed as she cradled her injured arm. Some of the more inebriated men were making unseemly comments about what she and Jack might have been doing.

Her arm was throbbing. She bit her lip, trying not to cry out. She wanted to find somewhere away from the ribald comments.

Ruby appeared without her usual smile. 'What a ker-fuffle! I've got your coat, Hannah, and Betty's finding your handbag and then we can be on our way. We'll go out the side door; you don't look too clever I can tell you. Did that Jack take liberties?'

'No, it was an accident. I think I've hurt my arm really badly. I feel very peculiar. I need fresh air before I faint.'

The thought of the further embarrassment gave her the strength to thread her way through the laughing crowd in to the blessed peace of the deserted corridor. Ruby's arm was around her waist - without it she would have collapsed. Her legs were shaking, she felt sick, and there was something seriously wrong with her right arm. When she tried to move it a horrible pain shot through her and she gasped out loud.

'Ruby, I think I'm going to be sick, I must get outside.'

'Bleedin' Nora! Come on, I've got you safe.'

Several horrible minutes later the retching was over; Hannah felt awful but at least the nausea had gone.

'We better get you back inside, there's no way you're going to ride back in your state. Boothroyd's not going to be best pleased with us, I can tell you.'

'I don't want to be a nuisance but I do need to sit down and get a sling for my arm.'

Betty arrived her torch flickering in one hand. 'Here,

Hannah, lean on me, we'll get you inside. I've told Joan you're not too good.'

Inside someone had lit the oil lamp. To her astonishment she was met by Jack and another unidentified airman. 'Betty says you've injured your arm, I've got Hugh Donnelly here, he's our medic. He'll examine you.' His tone was brisk; kind but impersonal. He stepped forward as if to assist but Betty spoke sharply to him.

'Thanks, but we can manage. Move yerself, this passage is too narrow to get past.'

Immediately he flattened himself against the wall apparently unbothered by the comment. 'You'll have to stay here tonight, they've got rooms, I've spoken to Joan and she's getting one ready for you. We'll explain what's happened, tell him you fell because of the blackout.' Betty said sympathetically. 'Rotten bad luck, but at least you won't have to clean the pigsty for a while.'

From somewhere Hannah found the strength to smile. 'Always a silver lining. I'm going to need my handbag and shoes. I'm not safe in these heels at the moment.'

Betty held up the sturdy brogues and the dropped handbag. 'Got them already. We'll have to get off soon, there's a nasty nip in the wind and we're not exactly dressed for warmth tonight.'

With a chorus of farewells the girls pedalled away leaving her alone with two men, one of whom she barely knew and one who was a complete stranger. She had no choice; she had to go with them. Jack made no attempt to assist her, but walked by her side. It was a comfort to have him close by. She re-entered the pub through the kitchen door. Mrs Stock was waiting.

'There you are, ducks, I've made you a nice, strong cup of tea with plenty of sugar. Just the ticket when you've had a nasty shock.'

Jack pulled out a chair and guided her in to it. 'I'll leave you to it, Doc, I'll be in the bar if you need me.'

'Let me have a look at this arm, young lady.' Dr Donnelly was older than the other airmen, probably nearer thirty than twenty. She heard his shocked gasp. 'Crickey! This is a very nasty break. I can put on a temporary splint but it's straight to hospital for you. No tea, this is going to need manipulation under anaesthetic.'

Chapter Three

The landlady removed the mug from Hannah's grasp. 'Sorry, ducks, the doctor knows what he's talking about. I'll go through and see if I can organise a lift.'

'Mr Boothroyd might well sack me; he won't keep me on the farm if I can't do my share. He'll want another land girl.'

'He'll do no such thing, miss, your job will be there when you're better. You can stay here if you like until you can work again.'

Hannah was touched by her kindness. 'I'll go back to the cottage, thank you, Mrs Stock, I can cook and tidy for Ruby and Betty and do quite a few things with one hand.'

'The offer still stands; you might change your mind. You could help me out behind the bar in exchange for your keep.'

That was different, if she didn't have to pay she'd prefer to be here in relative comfort than at Pond Farm. 'In which case, I'd love to stay, if you're quite sure I won't be in the way.'

'Be nice to have a bit of company as my old man's away.'

Dr Donnelly interrupted, patting Hannah on the shoulder. 'Grit your teeth, young lady, this is going to hurt. I have to stabilise the break before you can travel. It's only three miles to Saffron Walden, but I don't want to risk further damage.'

She closed her eyes and braced herself. The excruciating agony made her stomach churn, but concentrating on not being sick took her mind off what was being done to her fractured forearm.

'There, all done. Brave girl—that must have hurt like the dickens. Breathe slowly, the nausea and dizziness will pass.'

Mrs Stock spoke to the doctor. 'Jack's gone to borrow a vehicle, ducks, he'll be back in no time.'

As promised he returned and insisted he'd take her to hospital. 'After I've got you settled, Hannah, I'll nip to Pond Farm and tell the girls what's going on, they can pack you a bag. I'll bring it in first thing tomorrow.'

'I don't know why you're putting yourself out, you only met me this evening. But I appreciate your help, I promise I'll make it up to you…'

His eyebrows disappeared under the brim of his cap, his wicked grin told her she'd said something inappropriate. She was too tired and uncomfortable to explain.

With her left arm in one sleeve of her coat and her right arm supported in a sling he guided her through the deserted bar. The blackout curtain was back in place but the ceiling would need some repair. Apart from her injury the incident might never have happened. He ushered her in to the passenger seat of a small car and tucked a rug around her.

'Doc says you're in shock, that's why you're cold. Joan's bringing out a hot water bottle, you'll be much better then.'

She was considerably warmer than she'd been all day. Her teeth stopped chattering long before he pulled up in front of the General Hospital.

*

Monday morning she was released, her arm in snowy white plaster and no longer painful. Jack had brought her suitcase the day before and she'd dressed in warm slacks, blouse and thick cardigan. She sat in the freezing foyer glancing at the clock. He was late. There hadn't been an op last night, she'd been awake much of the time and would have heard the planes flying over.

A dilapidated van lurched to a halt outside and he jumped out. 'Sorry I'm late, Hannah, I had trouble borrowing a vehicle. I'm afraid this is all I could get, I've only got it for an hour - Jimmy's got a job on later this morning.'

Laughing she reached down to pick up her case but he grabbed it first. 'I don't care what I travel in and I've no idea who Jimmy is.'

He tossed her case in to the back and slammed the doors. By the time he'd done that she was safely installed in the front seat.

'Jimmy's the local builder, he's in great demand at the moment.'

'The aerodrome was bombed earlier but I didn't know civilians had been involved.'

'Unfortunately some bombs went astray and several houses were hit. He's not just repairing bomb damage, you wouldn't believe how many people back in to houses and that sort of thing because of the blackout.' He changed gear noisily. 'Then there's the railings to be collected - he's always busy.'

She giggled. 'I'm not surprised there are accidents - look at me?' The van swerved and she was thrown against the side jarring her good shoulder. 'I know you're in a hurry but please slow down, I don't want to break my other arm.'

'Sorry, I've not got the hang of this gearbox. It's easier flying then driving this old rust bucket.'

He ground to a standstill outside the pub a few minutes later. She was glad to get out; the bouncing had made her queasy. She leant against the side breathing deeply waiting for her head to clear. She might have several more days of this whilst the anaesthetic cleared her system. Thank goodness she wasn't going back to the farm.

'Here you are, come in, ducks, I expect you're half starved. Hospital food's no good for an invalid.' Mrs Stock nodded to Jack. 'Give us the case, love, you get on, Jimmy will be wanting to get to work.'

'Thanks, Joan. I'll be in this evening to see you, Hannah, unless something crops up.' With a cheery wave he drove off without waiting for a reply.

'Do you think they'll go out tonight Mrs Stock? Isn't it too foggy to fly?'

'That's enough of the Mrs Stock, call me Joan like everyone else does. If the fog clears they might go, but they were out Saturday night. I reckon they deserve a day off.'

Hannah's stomach lurched again. She hadn't heard the planes leave; she must have been too drowsy after her operation. 'Did we lose anyone?'

Joan shook her head. 'No, they all returned safely. It's good for business being close to the base but it's heartbreaking seeing young men disappear forever.' With the suitcase swinging from one hand Joan led her inside. 'Mind you,' she called, 'the squadrons are moving about the place like nobody's business and I pretend those boys have just been moved somewhere else.'

No more was said about missing airmen. Hannah wanted to believe the majority would turn up after the war. She was left to unpack, Joan had offered to do it for her but she'd refused. She needed to be more adept at doing things one-handed, after all there must be servicemen managing with only one limb.

The room was at the front and overlooked the strip of grass. The village hall was next door and there was a row of cottages opposite. There was a pond between the pub and the hall. How many unwary airmen had fallen in that? She might see the airfield if she stood on a chair but decided against it. With her luck she'd fall off and break something else.

It didn't take long to put away her belongings. The surgeon had been emphatic she wasn't to return to work for several weeks. She prayed she wouldn't have outstayed her welcome by then. She wasn't going to be paid whilst she was idle. She had little money as no one could save on the miserly wages the land army gave.

She put her flannelette nightdress under the pillow and smoothed back the pink candlewick bedspread. The room was cold, but a fire was ready in the grate and she would light this at bedtime. One thing about blackout curtains, they kept the heat in and the draughts out. There was a chamber pot under the bed and a candle and matches on the bedside table.

The White Hart didn't open at lunchtimes during the week so she wouldn't be needed in the bar until the evening. She was quite looking forward to helping out. She couldn't pull pints but she could collect dirty glasses and empty ash trays.

She buttoned her cardigan and headed for the stairs. The building must be over a hundred years old; she wasn't good at history but beams and wobbly walls usually meant the place was ancient.

The delicious smell of frying bacon wafted along the passageway; all she had to do was follow her nose to the kitchen. The door was open and Joan was serving up.

'I hope you're hungry, I've done you two rashers and an egg. Would you like mushrooms and fried bread as well?'

'Yes please. I've not had bacon for ages and I love mushrooms, I've been picking them in the fields recently.'

'Would you credit it, Mary Boothroyd fetched in your ration book and a lovely basket of eggs, mushrooms and vegetables. Wasn't that kind of her? Not a bit like her old man.'

'No, you're right. She scuttles about the farm hardly daring to say boo to the geese. Sometimes she's got a black eye. I think he mistreats her.'

'He does, far too free with his fists that one. He wasn't like that before their Alfie was lost at Dunkirk.' Joan shook her head. 'Took it real bad, both of them did. Mary used to be in and out of the village most days, always quiet but well liked and a ready smile for everyone.'

'How sad, no wonder he's so grumpy.'

Joan insisted she spent the afternoon resting upstairs with the fire alight. Tea was at five o'clock so they were ready to open at six. Tonight she would be an observer and remain on the customers' side.

She was wearing the same bottle green slacks as earlier, the only addition being a smudge of bright red lipstick. The fires were lit so the chill had gone from the public bar, the one the service personnel used. The locals used the lounge bar, at least the older folk did.

'Light the fire in the lounge, ducks, I don't suppose many will come in, it being a Monday, but you never know. Take one of the lamps from the sideboard. I'll unlock the doors then go round and check the blackout.'

The smaller room was freezing; the weather had turned nasty for the end of October. She was dreading the winter months; Betty and Ruby had said the last girl left because she couldn't cope with working in several degrees of frost. The spring and summer were lovely but when the nights got short and there was frost and snow on the ground field work was hard.

The crackle of kindling meant she could go and see what else she could do. The battered piano in the main bar beckoned her, she couldn't play properly with one hand but she could run her fingers across the keys. The piano was the only thing she missed from her former life; music had been her solace when things were difficult.

She unfolded the lid and ran her left hand across the keys. Perhaps she'd play one of the catchy modern tunes everyone was humming, *Run Rabbit Run* was a favourite of hers and the melody was simple. She tinkled through a selection of tunes before replacing the lid as a customer arrived.

The door behind the curtain opened. She stood up. Where was Joan? The heavy black material moved and Jack appeared.

'Are you open? I know the door's unlocked but it's not quite six o'clock.'

Seeing him without a press of people emphasised his height, somehow he'd seemed less formidable surrounded by others. She smiled, for some reason nervous. 'We're ready, but Joan's not here and I can't really do anything just yet.'

He tossed his coat on to a chair and removed his peaked cap. The uniform suited him; it made his eyes bluer. 'Not to worry, I came to see you. You looked knackered when I left you this morning.'

'I felt it, but as you see I'm fully restored, apart from my arm's in a sling. Come and sit by the fire, I shouldn't think anyone else will come in so early.'

There was no reason to feel uncomfortable; he'd done nothing to suggest he was not a gentleman. She smiled; he could hardly have made advances when she'd just broken her arm.

'Share the joke, Hannah, I could do with cheering up. The last op was my twentieth and we've another ten to go before we get some R&R. I'm the longest serving pilot in my squadron, every other bugger has gone for a burton.'

His sombre words banished any desire to laugh. She tried to lighten the mood. 'Remember, you said I'm your lucky talisman? As long as I'm here you'll get back safely.'

Joan rushed in to the bar exclaiming loudly when she saw Jack. 'You're an early one and no mistake. Just visiting, or would you like a drink? I've been changing the barrel so it's fresh on.'

He raised an eyebrow. 'Would you like something, Hannah? I don't want to drink on my own.'

'Just lemonade, or ginger beer - nothing alcoholic for me, thanks.'

Whilst he wandered across to collect the drinks she slipped in to the passage and doubled back to the kitchen. It was possible to see from the flicker of the range fire. She found the scissors and snipped off a curl. Taking a clean, white handkerchief from her pocket she folded the hair inside.

Jack and Joan were deep in conversation and hadn't noticed her absence. The cash register tinged and he turned with the glasses. The sound of laughter and loud male voices outside meant she didn't have long.

'Jack, I want you to put this in your pocket. It's your lucky charm.' She smiled and held out the cotton square. He stretched out and took it.

'What's this then?' He unfolded the material, his eyes widened when he saw what was there. Without a word being spoken he flipped the handkerchief closed undid the top button of his jacket. and placed the memento in an inside pocket. 'I shall treasure it; I'll never fly without it. Thank you, I can't tell you what it means to me.' His eyes were dark, his expression strange.

She was at a loss to know what to say, she'd no idea he'd take her gesture so seriously.

Obviously airmen were a superstitious lot. The pub door opened and several noisy customers bulged behind the blackout curtain. Pete and Dave burst in to the bar at the head of the group.

'There you are, might have known you'd sneaked off here to get a head start with our luscious new barmaid.' Pete strolled across to pat her on the shoulder - a gesture of sympathy rather than one of a hopeful admirer. 'Glad to see you back, Hannah, having you about the place will brighten our leisure hours.'

'I'm not working at the moment; Joan won't let me do anything today.'

'You can play us a tune.' Jack grinned. 'I heard you as I was parking the bike, doesn't matter if you can only use one hand, it's good enough for us to have a singsong later on.'

Dave arrived with two pints of beer. 'I bet you can sing as well, most pianists can carry a tune.'

She nodded. 'I was in the school choir, but I'm afraid I don't know the words of most of the popular songs, just the tunes.'

'We're going to have a game of darts, Jack. You taking on the winner?'

The evening sped by, despite it being a Monday the public bar was full. Hannah discovered there were a thousand aircrew, plus ground crew and a fair number of WAAF, at the base and the majority used the White Hart because of the beer.

Jack and his friends were happily playing darts which gave her the opportunity to study them. All three were good-looking but Jack stood out. Not only his height, but the fact that he was blond, blue-eyed and didn't have a moustache, made him more attractive in her opinion.

Dave was the quietest of the three, mousey hair and mud brown eyes, but his features were regular and his smile charming. She wasn't sure about Pete, over the evening he became brash and, if she was honest, just a little bit vulgar. But he was a good sort, and obviously thought the world of Jack. These were the men he relied on, his closest friends, and she was determined to like them for his sake.

As Jack was busy she collected glasses, emptied ashtrays and trimmed the wicks of lamps that needed it. Everyone was friendly, relaxed, enjoying the moment and not thinking about those that had died yesterday or those that might die tomorrow.

'Here, ducks, you've done enough tonight. You can help tidy up tomorrow morning, go and join your young man, he's looking a bit put out.'

'Honestly, Joan, Jack's just a friend.' Her landlady looked sceptical but said nothing. 'If you're sure, they've asked me to play a few tunes to round off the evening. Is that all right?'

'They know all the words and they'll drown out the piano anyway.' Joan winked. 'Don't let them sing the dirty versions, make your ears burn they would.'

After an hour of one-handed playing and riotous singing Hannah was more than ready to call it an evening. 'Jack, I'm sorry, I really have to stop now, I'm feeling a bit peculiar.'

Before anyone could protest he slammed the piano and whisked her in to the lounge bar. 'Sorry, I keep forgetting you've only just come out of hospital. Do you want me to help you upstairs?'

'No, thank you. I've enjoyed this evening, but I'm not used to crowds—and all the smoke and noise is a bit much.'

His brow creased. Thoughtfully he reached out and smoothed a stray curl from her forehead. She flinched away. 'Tell me, Hannah, how many bars have you been in to before this one?'

'Well … none …err … actually.'

'More cocktail parties and evenings at the Ritz, I expect? A bit of a comedown being in here with us, is it?' He was smiling, teasing, but was too close to the truth.

She stiffened. He had no right to criticise. 'My private life is exactly that, private. I haven't asked about *your* past. I thought everyone lived for today and that's what I want to do.' Her voice was sharp and his expression changed. Instantly contrite she grabbed his hand. 'I'm so sorry, I didn't mean to snap. I was desperately unhappy before I came here, that's why I don't want to talk about it.'

His eyes softened and his mouth curved, she noticed

laughter lines at the corner of his eyes.

'Sweetheart, I don't care who you are or where you come from, I knew the moment I saw you waving you were going to be part of my life.'

Thank God he made no attempt to kiss her; he would have done if she'd given him any encouragement. 'We've only known each other a few days but it's as if I've known you for ages.' She glanced up and was touched to see the uncertainty on his face.

'Will you be my girl now? My *someone special*?' He sensed her indecision. 'I don't expect ... well you know what I mean. It's just that I've really taken to you, can talk to you.' His lopsided smile made him appear younger than his years. 'Think of me as your big brother, nobody else needs to know we're not sleeping together.'

'I should think not! We've only known each other a couple of days. Where I come from girls don't ... well they just don't, not until they're engaged anyway.'

'That's all right then, we both know where we stand. You haven't answered my question, are you going to be my girl?'

'As long as you remember we're just friends, then I will. I have a photograph; next time you come in I'll give it to you if you like.'

'I'd love one, I can pin it in the cockpit. I don't suppose you've got two I can have? I can carry one in my wallet and show you off to the blokes. You're by far the best looking girl for miles; I'll be the envy of the squadron.'

He should leave; Joan would be through in a minute. 'Actually being your girlfriend will mean that *I* won't get pestered by anyone else and the local girls will stop making sheep's eyes at *you* every time you come in the bar.'

'Will it be okay for us to hold hands sometimes? If we don't it might look a bit odd.'

She moved away from him, her pleasure in the arrangement marred by his suggestion. 'No, I don't think so. Sorry,

I'm a convent girl and it goes against everything I've been taught' Flustered, she stumbled in to a chair and would have fallen but for his quick reactions. He released her arm immediately.

'Hannah, I give you my word I'll not do anything you don't want. I'm hoping when you get to know me you'll realise I'm not a bad chap and will want to hold my hand occasionally.'

'Thank you, I really do like you, it's me … not you. Maybe I'll feel differently in a week or two. But until then, I still want to be your girl.' She smiled up at him. 'If you were posted overseas I would write to every day, I promise.'

Joan appeared carrying the last of the dirty glasses. 'You still here, Jack? The others are waiting; if you don't hurry they'll go without you.'

Hannah didn't want to discuss anything with her landlady. She was already regretting her indiscretion to Betty the other night. Would her secret be all over their neighbourhood before the next dance?

*

Jack joined his friends who are waiting in a noisy huddle outside the pub. Not allowing them any time to make ribald comments, he pedalled furiously out of the village and up the hill that led to the 'drome. Pete and Dave were definitely the worse for wear and had difficulty keeping up with him.

At least they couldn't be scrambled unexpectedly, unlike the bods in the fighters. Johnny had told him on the QT that they would be out tomorrow night. Now he had a lock of Hannah's hair to keep him safe he was almost looking forward to it - as long as it wasn't in the middle of Germany again. Last time the ack-ack had been ferocious, the night fighters deadly; it was a miracle his squadron had returned in one piece.

Pete wobbled violently and disappeared in to the ditch. Neither he nor Dave bothered to stop and pull him out, Pete was an expert at extricating himself from the brambles.

'I like your new girl, Jack, not only smashing to look at but a bit of class as well. About time you settled for someone, give us poor sods a chance with the locals. None of them will look at us if they think they're in with half a chance with you.'

'I've been waiting for the right one, there's something about Hannah that makes her special. I can see I'm going to be doing a lot of extra peddling in future, you'll have to drink at The Fox on your own in future.'

'No such luck, you're not getting rid of us that easily. Pete and I play *follow our leader*, you know that. And anyway, The Fox might be a lot nearer but it doesn't have the added attraction of the village hall being next door.'

A furious rattling behind them meant Pete was catching up. 'Hey, you blighters, wait for me. You know I'm scared of the dark.'

They slipped in through the side gate, the sentry here was less likely to make a fuss if they were a trifle noisy. 'Looks like we're last in as usual. Whose turn is it to make the tea?'

Dave propped his bike next to several others before answering. 'Yours, Skip. I've got half a packet of biscuits left and I fancy cocoa tonight. I used the last of my ration to buy some this morning, cost me nine pence - but worth it.'

There were officers' servants to look after them, they could drag one of the unfortunate sods out of bed, but that wouldn't be fair. The small block, adjacent to their sleeping quarters, was quiet, no one else bothering to make themselves a late-night snack before falling in to bed.

It was almost midnight when Jack returned to his rooms; as a senior officer he had his own sitting room but rarely used it, preferring to sit in the mess with the others. Maybe they'd all sleep better if they were sharing accommodation like the ranks, had someone to talk to in the small hours. Both his mates were commissioned, Dave a pilot officer and Pete a flying officer; it wouldn't be long before Pete was made a flight lieutenant too. When that happened he would be offered his own kite, but Pete wouldn't go - they were a tight unit, there was only one thing that would separate them and he prayed that would never happen.

Chapter Four

Hannah slept well and woke before dawn. Habit made her scramble out and head for the wash stand, being careful not to get her plaster wet. She hadn't had to use the pot under the bed so that was one less thing to do.

With her candle in one hand she crept through the pub to the kitchen determined to get the range going and have breakfast ready before Joan came down. She could do most things that didn't involve water. The fingers on her right arm were an interesting shade of blue but seemed to work well enough.

With a tea cloth tucked around the plaster she riddled the ancient range and soon had it burning fiercely. Fortunately Joan had collected sufficient water for the morning; two full buckets stood in the scullery.

Less than an hour later the bar was polished, the floor swept and both fires ready to light. Her arm ached but not as badly as her back and shoulders did after a hard day picking brussels, or digging up turnips or mucking out the pigsty. The glasses were in the scullery, both kettles had boiled but she was waiting for Joan before making the tea.

She glanced at the clock above the fireplace in the kitchen - nearly seven o'clock. What time did her landlady get up? She'd venture outside and use the privy. Hopefully it wouldn't smell too bad first thing in the morning. It had better not be her job to empty *those* buckets.

By the time she returned Joan was there smiling broadly. 'My, you've been busy and no mistake. What a luxury to get up and find everything done and the kitchen lovely and warm. Come and sit down, the tea's brewed and we'll have that before I start breakfast.'

Two cups of tea later a plate of mushrooms and fried bread was placed in front of Hannah. 'Goodness, I shall be enormous by the time I return to Pond Farm if I eat as much as this every day.'

'You tuck in, ducks, you could do with a bit of meat on your bones. I'm making a couple of slices of toast for after, I've got some lovely marmalade to go with it. We have to use up every crumb nowadays so you'll be helping the war effort by eating my stale bread.'

She met several people on the way to the standpipe, this was a good place for the housewives to stand and have a bit of a gossip. One trip was all that was needed this morning but she would have to go down a couple of times before dark. She would check with Joan when was the quietest time.

At opening time she heard the roar of the bombers taking off; she counted to twelve but the planes kept coming. Both squadrons were in action tonight. Then there was distinctive sound of the fighters afterwards. Where were they going? Tonight was a big sortie; the Debfield squadrons would rendezvous with dozens of others somewhere. Sometimes more than two hundred bombers left England in one attack. The fighters escorted the bombers on their mission. She prayed they'd all return safely in the morning. Tonight was going to be long and sleepless.

*

The briefing room was tense. This was it. The heart stopping moment when the Group Captain announced tonight's destination. This was going to be a long hop, the fuel tanks were filled to capacity and rumour had it that they were going to bomb an industrial site in the heart of Germany.

The ripple of relief around the room, when they learnt they were going to Italy, was palpable. Flying over the Alps was a nightmare but the Italians were less committed to shooting down enemy planes than their German counterparts. Last time Jack had been there the anti-aircraft guns had stopped as his squadron flew overhead, the blighters had taken cover whilst the bombs were dropped, then the ack-ack had started again in a haphazard fashion as he beat a rapid retreat.

He grinned at his crew. 'Right – Turin here we come. A damn sight better than going to Germany.'

Pete shrugged in to his flying jacket and knotted his lucky scarf around his neck. 'It's a fine night, no fog and plenty of moonlight. We can sit back and enjoy the scenery for the next few hours.'

The meeting was breaking up and the bods were heading for their kites. There were the pre-flight checks to do before they got the signal to take off. Johnny waved at him and Jack told his friends he would join them on the perimeter.

'Jack, old bean, this is the big one. We rendezvous over Kent with the rest of the formation but make our own way home.'

'Roger that, Skip, be a walk in the park going to Italy.'

'That's the spirit, less likely to be casualties tonight unless some of the silly beggars get lost.'

'Are the Spits and Hurricanes coming?'

'They'll follow us across the Channel, then escort us back. Should be over by three o'clock, plenty of time for a kip before breakfast.'

Outside it was light enough not to bother with his torch. Jack exchanged a joke or two with the ground crew, who were standing by to remove the chocks, then scrambled aboard. It was a tight squeeze in the tiny cockpit, but he slid easily in to his space without treading on Dave's feet.

Pete was in the back checking the gun. 'Okay, you chaps, let's get this done, we're first off tonight.'

Having completed the routines he turned to the others. 'Let's hop down and have a cuppa, we won't get another decent one until we get back.' Jones handed round the mugs. 'Thanks, mate. The old girl sounds in good voice, you've done a grand job as usual.'

'Ta, Skip, don't want my favourite crew to go for a burton on my watch. I've put your flasks under the nav's seat, 'fraid it's spam in the sarnies. Reckon you'll have a nice clear run tonight.' He glanced over his shoulder as a jeep pulled up beside them.

The Group Captain had come to wish them well. It must be difficult knowing some of the blokes he exchanged greetings with might not return. Jack hoped he'd never have the unenviable task of writing to the sweetheart, mother or wife of a bloke who bought it.

He turned his wrist and saw it was almost time. 'Righty ho, put the fags out, we've to get a move on.'

In the gloom of the cabin he snapped his harness shut, no need to ask if the others were doing the same, they'd flown together too often for reminders to be necessary. He switched on, revved up and taxied round to the runway. His mouth was dry, his palms damp inside his gloves, but once he was airborne the excitement of flying would kick in and he'd be fine.

Up ahead he saw the green light from the airfield control, pushed the throttle open and the plane was tearing down the concrete. The nose lifted sweetly and the rest followed. They were safely up and on their way. At first there was desultory conversation, but soon that died away and the only noise in the cockpit was the drone of the engines.

His job was to make sure the six planes under his command stayed in formation, stragglers we're a sitting target for the ever watchful Messerschmitt. Crossing France was uneventful, no trouble from flak or fighters. The mountains below looked stunning; in the silvery light the snow-capped peaks glittered peacefully. A beautiful vista made a chap forget the real reason he was up there.

From behind him Pete called out glumly. 'Pity the poor buggers who have to bail out over this lot. They'd freeze before anyone found them.'

Jack chuckled. 'And there I was thinking how beautiful they were, trust you to spoil the moment.'

'Don't put the mockers on it, Pete, we've done this trip a couple of times, third time lucky and all that.'

Jack knew his flight engineer was superstitious, but then weren't they all? Hadn't he got a lock of hair in his shirt pocket to keep him safe? 'I never thought breaking one's arm could be a good thing, but Hannah's got a soft billet now. I hope it takes a long time for the medic to give her the all clear. Betty and Ruby told me they only get a weekend pass every six months, and then only if the farmer can spare them. At least we get time off when there's no op.'

'Those girls do work harder than us but they don't risk life and limb every time they pick up a hoe.'

The radio crackled and Johnny's voice prevented his reply. 'Almost there, we go in behind the Wellingtons, then drop your load and circle and head for home. Good luck to you all. See you in Blighty.'

No time to talk, Pete had to concentrate and give precise instructions until they were over the target area and could drop their bombs. Hardly seemed worth coming all this way with the small load they carried, but the powers that be obviously thought they needed every squadron involved tonight.

The Alps dropped away behind them. He had to descend

to 12,000 feet for the bombing run. This was the dodgy time, when the Italian gunners had the most chance of hitting them. They followed the planes in front, he dodged and weaved through the flak and on Pete's command pulled the lever. The plane shot in to the air as the weight dropped away but he was ready for it.

They were turning, hardly daring to believe they'd come through unscathed, when the plane lurched. They'd been hit. Pete was turning the air blue, thank God he was unhurt. Smoke and flames poured from the port engine. He knew the drill, reacted by instinct. Throttled back, feathered the engine and pressed the extinguisher button. The foam did the trick. The fire went out.

'Blimey, that was close. The radio's on the blink, Skip. We're going to have to find our own way home.'

'You're our navigator, Dave, it's up to you.' They were losing height; with one engine they couldn't fly over the peaks, they'd have to find their way through and hope to God they didn't hit anything. 'Okay, chaps, keep your eyes peeled. Pete you watch the port, Dave the starboard. As long as the moon stays out we've got a chance. Pete, start chucking anything we don't need. Dave, plot a course away from the highest mountains.'

A rush of freezing air indicated the escape hatch was open behind him. The plane jumped and rocked each time something was dumped. He stared ahead at the formidable range, what had looked stunning on the way over now seemed a waiting death trap. He would have to keep adjusting height, weaving and slipping left and right on command, jerking the control column to keep them away from the cliffs and outcrops of rock.

'Ready, Skip, I dumped the flares, but I thought I'd hang on to the parachutes, just in case.'

'Bloody, ha ha! Always the comedian, Pete. Here we go. All aboard for the skylark!'

'Gordon Bennet! That was too close for comfort,' Jack said as he yanked the control column for the umpteenth time. 'How much further, Dave?'

'No idea, all this swerving and dodging makes it damn near impossible to pinpoint our position.'

Jack knew one slip on his part would mean instant death for them all. The ravines were never ending, several times he narrowly missed smashing in to the sides. Even a wing tip touching the wall and it would be over. Then he remembered he had his lucky talisman in his pocket, his spirits lifted, he knew they'd emerge safely on the other side of the range.

There was no time for Dave to re-plot their course, he was too busy shouting instructions. Jack thanked God at least he could see far enough ahead to know when to climb to avoid a wall of rock. He was beginning to relax when Pete screamed a warning.

'Skipper, right ahead, we're heading for a cliff face. Climb, climb, climb.'

Frantically Jack banked to starboard lifting the port wing, the end almost scraped the massive outcrop. His breath hissed through his teeth. He wasn't sure how much more the kite would take before the second engine spluttered out.

'Look, open sky. We've bloody done it! Well done, Skip.' Dave collapsed in to his seat and immediately re-plotted their course.

'That felt like eternity, the longest twenty minutes of my life. How much fuel we got left, Skip?'

Jack tapped the dial. 'Not enough, Pete, but with luck we'll get to Blighty before we have to land. We could all do with a cuppa; Pete, will you do the honours?'

Somehow he nursed the plane across France; the worst bit was crossing the Channel, if they'd ditched without flares there was little hope of them being picked up. They flew over Kent and were almost at Debfield when, from nowhere, three German fighters attacked.

Not now! They'd got this far, surely they were going to reach home safely? If the Spits didn't come to their rescue they'd be shot down. He couldn't risk it. He'd take the damaged kite in, but he wouldn't let his crew go down with him.

'Pete, Dave, bail out. Don't argue—that's an order.'

Chapter Five

The plane lurched sickeningly. Pete, who was snapping shut his harness, stumbled and crashed to one side. Dave said nothing, just snatched up his parachute and buckled it on. When they were ready he turned and gripped Jack's shoulder.

'Good luck, mate, we'll see you in the pub for a pint later.'

There was no time for further conversation, the tap-tap-tap of the machine guns ripping through the fuselage sent his friends diving for the escape hatch. Where the hell were the Spitfires when you wanted them? The control stick jerked sideways twice. Thank God! Pete and Dave would be safe; all he had to do was ditch this crate and pray to God he didn't kill himself in the process.

There was no time to search the sky for the tell-tale white of the canopies. If they hadn't bailed out when they did it would have been too late, they'd have been too low for the chutes to open. The Germans were still firing. The plane rocked violently as another burst of gunfire smashed in to the tail.

Then three Spitfires roared past. About bloody time - at least he could concentrate on finding a field to land in. He'd not reach Debfield - the best he could do was avoid any trees or houses. The one remaining engine coughed and died. He'd run out of fuel. The ground was rushing towards him. He throttled back and raised the flaps. The landing gear refused to drop. His vision blurred. He recovered. A belly flop might be safer. If the wheels hit something the plane would somersault.

He saw a ploughed field bordered by thick hedges, no large trees visible, thank the Lord. With an empty tank there was less likelihood of going up in flames. He braced himself and hung on for grim death. The crate dropped the last few feet like a stone. The nose crumpled. The port wing dipped and dug in to the earth. With a ghastly ripping sound it tore away and the plane slewed crazily to the right. For a moment he was surrounded by silence then his world went black.

*

Three fighters screamed overhead. Hannah fell out of bed and stumbled across the bedroom.

There was enough light from the embers for her to pull the blackout away. She'd have to open the window. Flicking the catch across she heaved and it grated up.

There were six fighters, their outlines silvered by moonlight. The sky was torn apart by streams of white light; it would have been spectacular if these weren't bullets flying in the darkness.

Which were English and which German? The noise overhead was deafening. The planes swooped and dived like huge, demented birds—impossible to see who was winning.

Suddenly a surge of orange surrounded one of the planes and it spiralled its way earthwards. Immediately two broke away and raced in to the night pursued by the other three; a German plane had been hit and the three Spitfires had gone after the remaining Messerschmitts. There'd been no parachute. The pilot had had no chance to bail out; she watched his slow descent and saw a yellow flash as the noise of the crash reached her.

She pulled down the window and replaced the blackout. Although Germans were vilified as Nazis, as evil men with no compassion, they weren't all Storm Troopers or SS. Every pilot was somebody's son, brother or husband.

No point in returning to bed; she would get up, do her chores and go for a bike ride before breakfast. Maybe she'd go to the base and check everyone had returned safely. The sentry on the gate was bound to know.

She crept out the back way. The village was eerily silent, no one fetching water, feeding chickens or queuing up for their daily provisions. This was the time of day she loved best; the world felt new, she had it all to herself.

A slight sound startled her as she removed her bike from the shed. She looked down - two beady yellow eyes peered back. Only a rat - nothing for her to worry about. One of her jobs on the farm was to catch and kill the rats. She'd set some traps when she got back.

Something prompted her to turn towards the coppice where the fighter had crashed. No doubt the officious home guard captain was there with his men; if he was, she would find another route. There was something unnerving about Captain Turner. When he and his men had marched through the farm Betty told her to give him a wide berth, that he was unhinged, something to do with his experiences in the first war. The man was fanatical about rooting out traitors and fifth columnists. He'd shot a German pilot, attempting to surrender, in cold blood.

She couldn't see between the high hedges but when she turned onto a farm track and pedalled towards the thin column of smoke things were brighter. The crashed plane was empty – but then she saw a flicker of light inside the cockpit. It exploded and burnt like a beacon. Someone would arrive to investigate. They'd think the pilot had died in the fire.

Where was he? An image of her brother lying helpless on the ground flicked through her mind.

Had someone helped *him*? She decided to find the missing pilot. If Captain Turner and his men found him first he would probably be shot.

It would be full light soon and she didn't want to be seen near the crashed Messerschmitt, she'd spent too long here already. After breakfast she'd tell Joan she was going to see Betty and Ruby and pack sandwiches and a flask of tea for lunch. Her spare nightdress would make excellent bandages. She'd find a couple of sacks and take those with her. They'd do as blankets if she found the man. She'd stay with him until someone came along who could be trusted not to kill him.

She reached the pub without seeing any sign of interest in the crash site. The longer the airman had before anyone turned up the better. There were several disused barns in the vicinity, maybe the pilot was there.

She dumped her bicycle in the shed, grabbed a bucket from the scullery and ran down to the standpipe. She had no intention of lying, if asked directly if she'd been out of the village she'd tell the truth. Hopefully Joan would think she had her coat on because she'd been fetching water.

'There you are, ducks, I've told you there's no need to do that, what with your bad arm and all. Here, let me take it, you look worn out. I'll not have your young man saying I'm making you work too hard.'

The bucket changed hands slopping icy water in to Hannah's shoe. 'Gosh, that was cold. I'll nip upstairs and change my socks, Joan. I'm going to Pond Farm to see my friends today, if you don't mind.'

Her sock wasn't particularly wet, she'd used the excuse to return to her bedroom and stuff her haversack with things she might need. She hated deceiving Joan, but wasn't sure she'd understand her motives.

Over breakfast they talked about the night raid, Hannah apologised for using up some of the precious cocoa and milk. 'I couldn't sleep until I heard the fighters take off. I counted everyone back, at least I think I did.' She didn't mention anything about the dogfight—better to appear ignorant.

'You take whatever you want, I've got your ration book and Mary hasn't been using all your coupons. I'll get a lovely bit of liver for tea tonight. What are you going to do for lunch?'

'I'd like to take a picnic to share with the girls. I need my gumboots and a couple of other things as well. Are you sure you can spare the bread and cheese and things?' She shifted uncomfortably, finding it harder to lie than she'd expected. Joan beamed and gestured expensively towards the pantry. 'Help yourself, ducks. Why don't you make yourself a nice flask of tea as well? Take a decent slice of cake and some apples to go with your sandwiches. It's hungry work on the fields.'

On the pretext of finding sacks to sit on Hannah rummaged through the shed. Her haversack hung heavily over her shoulder and the basket in front of the handlebars was bulging with goodies. Pond Farm was in the right direction so she'd call in for a quick chat and thank Mrs Boothroyd for the produce then go on her search. Then if Joan asked, Ruby and Betty could confirm she'd been with them.

After wobbling dangerously over the potholes she gave up and hid her bike behind the hedge. She'd walk the last mile to the farm. The sound of the pigs squealing and Betty swearing at them made her smile.

'Betty, Ruby, I've come to see how you're getting on without me.'

Betty's red face appeared over the wall of the pigsty. 'Blimey, Hannah, didn't expect to see you out here. Have you walked all the way from the village?'

'No, but I couldn't manage the ruts one-handed so abandoned my bike in the hedge. Has Boothroyd found anyone else?'

'Not yet, but someone from the pool is supposed to come today. She'll not stay here, she'll cycle from her digs. How long's it going to be before you get your plaster off?'

'Several weeks, I hope Mr Boothroyd takes me back as I won't be able to do as much heavy work as before, not initially anyway.'

'Can't stop, too bleedin' much to do with you away. Ruby's in the milking parlour with Arthur, I'll tell her you called in. We'll come for a drink on Saturday night if we're not too knackered.'

'Good, I'm just going to pop in and say thank you to Mrs Boothroyd for the basket and then get some things from my room. I'm going to have a picnic somewhere.'

'Lucky for some! Fancy a broken arm giving you a life of Riley. TTFN - must get on or I'll be for the high jump. He wants me to start pulling leeks after this; bet you're glad you're not here.'

'Actually, I really miss you both. I love working on the land. I'll be back just as soon as I'm allowed to.'

Her duty visit accomplished she hurried back down the lane to recover her bike. This was awkward and heavy to push with so much weight in the basket and by the time she reached the end of the lane she was beginning to regret her impulsive decision.

Puffed and hot in her thick, land army jacket she dismounted on the brow of a hill to look round. She wiped the worst of the perspiration from her face and stared across the empty fields.

There were two possibilities; the first, a large Dutch barn with half the tiles missing; the second, a building tucked away behind a hedge with only a glimpse of the red roof visible.

This would be a better place to hide but it was more than

a mile from the crash site. Could a wounded man have staggered that far in the darkness? She would try there first.

Keeping close to the hedges where she was less likely to be seen, she pedalled precariously around the perimeter of the first field. She couldn't take her bike any further; she would hide it in a ditch and carry everything. As she was pushing her way through a particularly spiteful patch of nettles she heard the distant sound of a truck.

She froze. Was it coming in her direction? Had the authorities realised the pilot had escaped? If she was caught helping him she'd be arrested. Her stomach lurched. Would she be considered a traitor and hung? Her knees gave way and she flopped to the ground pressing in to the hedge in the hope she'd be invisible.

Her heart thudding drowned everything else. This was ridiculous! If she was seen she'd say she was enjoying the fresh air; until she made contact with the German there was nothing anyone could prove.

Her breathing calmed. The truck came no closer; the engine noise faded. She brushed debris from her slacks and gathered her dropped parcels. The roof of the ramshackle building wasn't far ahead and was well hidden amongst the overgrown hawthorns and sloe bushes. Here was an ideal place to hide.

She was approaching from the rear, her feet silent in the soft mulch that lined the ditch. If anyone was inside they wouldn't hear her. When she was a few yards away she stopped. Should she call out? No—better not. She'd reconnoitre before going in.

Her arm was aching. She dumped everything and crept closer to peer through a crack in the weather boarding. The sun didn't reach this small corner of the field, the high hedges and overhanging trees kept the building more or less in permanent shadow.

She listened - only birdsong and the distant chug-chug

of a tractor. She found a knot hole in the boards. Was it empty? Wasn't that a man up against the far wall? He was almost invisible amongst the ancient hay.

There was a door of sorts. She could step through without alerting the sleeping pilot. As she was climbing in it occurred to her this man might not be pleased to see her. He could be a Nazi. Half in-half out she froze.

She wouldn't wake him, just leave the food and other things outside. She must have been mad to even think of accosting an enemy. Too late - the shape moved and she found herself staring down the barrel of a revolver.

'Put your hands above your head, Fraulein, or I will shoot you.'

Chapter Six

Hannah clung to the door frame. Her bowels threatened to loosen, her head spun and she slid to the ground. The German airman was on his knees beside her when she opened her eyes, his face pale, his expression no longer threatening.

'I beg your pardon, young lady, it was not my wish to frighten you so much. Here, see, I have put my weapon down.'

The man spoke almost accentless English, his voice pleasant, he was no Nazi murderer. Slowly she pushed herself up on her elbows. She felt more ridiculous than scared. 'I'm all right now; it was the shock of having a gun pointed at me. I saw your plane come down last night and I've come to help you.'

'Kurt Schumann at your service, Fraulein.'

She smiled, her terror gone. From the light filtering through the door she saw a young man, about twenty five, fairly tall but slimly built. His hair was dark, which was odd because his eyebrows were fair. Good grief! There was blood on his head. No wonder he was pale.

'You've a nasty gash on your head. Do you have other injuries? I've basic first aid training and can deal with your cut but if you've anything worse I shan't know what to do.'

'I believe I have a few cracked ribs. Might I ask, Miss Hannah, exactly what were your intentions coming to the rescue of your enemy? I take it you are quite alone out here?'

Her throat tightened. Why was he asking these questions? Did he mean her harm?

'It is far too late, young lady, to be worrying about your personal safety. If I had wished to shoot you I would have done so ten minutes ago, I had a perfect opportunity when you were creeping along the hedge.'

Annoyance replaced her nervousness. 'In which case, Herr Schumann, why did you frighten me half to death?'

'I wished to give you a salutary lesson. I hope you will not put yourself in danger again. The men I flew with last night would have had no compunction. You would now be another casualty of war.'

'Well, I'm not and you're not, so I'll get my things and start cleaning your head. I've bandages which should help your ribs.'

Not waiting to hear his reply she scrambled to her feet and hurried in to the sunshine. He'd been right to frighten her, she shouldn't have come. She ought to have reported him to the local constable and relied on him to keep the man safe from the home guard.

She was committed now, could hardly abandon Herr Schumann. Whilst she gathered up her belongings she considered the pilot. He was as far away from the accepted idea of a German as she was. He was courteous, spoke English fluently and was obviously well-educated.

'I've brought a flask of tea, some sandwiches, cake and a few apples. I've also got a bottle of water. This will keep you going for today. I couldn't find blankets, but I've got three sacks, they'll have to do.'

He was on his feet supporting himself against the wall. He nodded, would probably have clicked his heels if he'd been well enough. 'Thank you, Miss Hannah, I am most grateful for your assistance but at a loss to think why you should wish to help me.'

She had better tell him what to expect if the home guard appeared. 'I'm afraid Captain Turner, of the home guard, is deranged. He's already shot one German pilot who wished to surrender. I know he would do the same to you.'

'So, you have evil men on your side as well. I was warned I would be summarily executed if found but thought that scaremongering. We are supposed to shoot ourselves rather than be captured.'

Hannah placed the sack by the door and gently guided him to it. 'Mr Schumann, if you sit in the light I'll do what I can. Your cut needs stitching, I've brought my sewing things. Do you think you can stand the pain?'

'I should prefer the discomfort to bleeding to death. Could I have a cup of tea before you start?'

She supported him until he was safely down. After he'd drunk his tea he nodded and closed his eyes. She tipped some of the water onto a cloth and investigated the gash. He flinched a couple of times as she put in three clumsy stitches but remained silent.

'There, I expect you'll have a scar but it should heal. It's stopped bleeding. I'm going to put a bandage around your head to keep it clean; an old barn is hardly the best place for an injury like this.'

Her face was inches from his. He opened his eyes and for a second he looked familiar. Golly! He could be a distant cousin of Jack's with his fair hair, blue eyes and regular features.

Admittedly the colours were slightly different. Jack had sky-blue eyes and corn coloured hair, this German pilot was a paler facsimile, as if the brightness was washed out somehow. Embarrassed to be caught staring she shuffled back, busying herself in her haversack to cover her red face.

His pale blue eyes darkened. 'I heard the plane explode, I was lying in a ditch half a mile away. I was hoping they would think I'd died and not search for me.'

'Well, I don't think anyone's looking at the moment. I'm supposed to be having a picnic but the sun's gone in and no one will believe I stayed out all day.'

He pointed to a pile of old straw near his bed. 'Please, Fraulein, will you not be seated so we can talk? I have not had the opportunity to practice my English for several years.'

'I was wondering about that; were you a lecturer in English before the war?'

'How intelligent you are, young lady. I was indeed a professor of English at Munich University. I have been obliged to apologise many times since this terrible war started.' He closed his eyes, obviously in some pain.

'I've brought you some paper and a couple of pencils, I thought you might like to sketch or something. Hang on a minute; they're still in my haversack.'

He watched her tidy up, putting everything within arm's reach, but remained quiet.

'Fraulein, what is going to happen to me? I cannot stay here for long and it will go badly for you if anyone discovers you have been of assistance to me.'

'I'll speak to the local constable; once an official report has been made I don't think Captain Turner will risk harming you.'

He shook his head. 'You do not understand what I have said to you. You cannot be involved in this; somehow you must send this policeman in my direction without revealing you have been here.' He looked carefully at the pile of food and other items she had left for him. 'Is there anything here that could be traced back to you, Fraulein?'

She checked, certain even the paper and pencils were those that could be bought at any stationers. 'Nothing here to worry about, Herr Schumann, and if you eat all the food and bury the bottle and paper bags no one will know. The sacks could well have been left in the barn ...' her voice trailed away as she stared at his smart new bandage. He could hardly have stitched up his cut himself and the cloth was quite definitely torn from a nightdress.

'I see you have finally grasped the seriousness of the situation. I should never have let you dress my wound; I have put you in grave danger.'

'Too late to worry about it, I'll think of something on the way back, don't worry ...' she couldn't keep calling him Herr Schumann, he was obviously an officer as there were chevrons on his uniform. 'What's your rank, I should like to be able to report you correctly.'

'Hauptsturmfuher Schumann, I believe that it is the equivalent of an English Flight Lieutenant.'

'Goodbye, Flt Lt Schumann, I doubt we'll meet again. Good luck.'

He pushed himself upright and gripped her hand within both of his. For some reason she wasn't repelled by the contact. 'You are a very special young lady, Fraulein Hannah. A brave and resourceful one, I have no wish to put you at further risk.'

She hurried out. She hated goodbyes and prayed he would be safe until she could point the dim-witted PC Smith in his direction. She had scarcely parked her bike and collected her gumboots and bits and pieces from the basket when Joan rushed out from the kitchen.

'There you are, thank goodness you've come back early.' She seemed unable to continue, she was holding back tears. A terrible weight settled on Hannah's chest. Something dreadful had happened and it must be something to do with the German pilot.

*

The distinctive rattle of the tea trolley dragged Jack from his semiconscious state. It felt as though someone had drilled a hole in his shoulder. If he moved his head blinding pain shot through it.

'Ah, Flt Lt Rhodes, back in the land of the living I see.' The nurse gently lifted his wrist to check his pulse. 'You have concussion and a nasty injury to your shoulder. However, the good news is you will make a full recovery.'

If he kept his eyes closed and his head down he could manage to force his wandering wits in to some sort of order. 'How long?'

'You've been here since this morning; it's three o'clock in the afternoon. Would you like a nice cup of tea?'

He would, but the thought of moving his head in order to swallow it made him refuse. 'No, thank you. Any visitors?'

'I believe your Wing Commander came in an hour ago.' The nurse smoothed out his sheets and left him alone with his thoughts. Why hadn't Pete or Dave come? Perhaps they couldn't get a lift; Ely *was* a long way from the base. But when Dave had a prang on his bike a few months ago he and Pete had made the journey.

He frowned and regretted it. They would be along later moaning because he couldn't fly and they'd have to join another crew until he was fit.

When he woke later Wing Co was sitting at his bedside. He didn't smile. Jack edged himself upright; he wanted to look Gerald in the eye when he got the bad news.

'There's no easy way to say this, old chap, Pete and Dave bought it last night. Those bastard Germans gunned them down after they bailed out. It's not your fault. You did the right thing. You couldn't know they would have survived if they'd stayed in the crate.'

'Both of them? Dead? I don't believe it. Pete and Dave gone for a burton?'

The Wing Co nodded. 'Our Spits got all three of them,

they didn't live to gloat.'

Jack turned his head away. Blokes died, got shot down, crashed … but he'd never heard of anyone being machine gunned after they'd jumped. Whatever the Wing Co said, the deaths of two of the best friends were on *his* conscience. Tit-for-tat; he would forget about playing fair. This was a dirty war and if he ever came face-to-face with a German he'd put a bullet through his head without a qualm.

'I've written to the families but I expect they'd like to hear from you as well. You'll be *hors de combat* for a while. The medics tell me they're keeping you in for a few more days. Do you have somewhere to go to recuperate?'

'I'll put up at the pub in Debfield, Mrs Stock has plenty of rooms. Thank you for coming to tell me personally … much appreciated, sir.'

As he lay there his grief was driven out by an ice cold anger against the murderers. He'd get himself fit, be back in the air soon but ask to be transferred to a fighter squadron. He'd trained on smaller planes, a couple of solo flights and he'd be proficient.

Flying a Spitfire would mean he could devote the rest of the war to avenging his friends, shoot down every German in his sights. The jolly nurse reappeared, this time with his medication and the cup of tea he'd refused earlier.

'Nurse, where am I?'

'This is the RAF hospital at Ely. You were brought over by ambulance after the medic at the base had temporarily patched you up.'

'No, I meant what ward am I in?'

'Ward 3; now - drink your tea - you need to keep up your fluids.'

*

'Is it Jack? Please, don't tell me he's dead.'

'No, ducks, he's injured but not too bad. Pete and Dave were killed last night. Come in, I'll get you a nice hot cuppa, you've gone a bit pale looking.'

Joan took her elbow and guided her inside; she collapsed on a kitchen chair and dropped her head in to her hands. She was glad Jack wasn't dead, but Pete and Dave were his best friends, he'd be distraught at losing them. A hot mug was pushed between her fingers. The sweet liquid revived her, she straightened, was ready to discover what happened.

'How did they die? Was there a crash?'

Joan's expression changed to fury. 'You won't believe it; the whole village is shocked rigid. Them evil beggars shot Pete and Dave when they were on their way down. Fancy that! To kill those poor boys when they were a few yards from safety!'

Hannah felt sick. The two German pilots with Flt Lt Schumann were responsible. 'Did our fighters get them?'

'They did, one came down a couple of miles from here but the other two were shot down over the North Sea. Good thing too, any German that bails out around here in future … well I don't fancy his chances, do you? Captain Turner won't be criticised now if he finishes any of those blighters off.'

Hannah mumbled a reply, gripping the mug to stop her fingers trembling. The gentle pilot hiding in the barn would never have done anything so horrible. Hadn't he told her the men he'd been flying with would have shot her without compunction? What was she going to do? Until the furore died down Flt Lt Schumann's life would be forfeit.

'There, ducks, don't take on so. I warned you, you have to get used seeing our brave boys disappear. There's a war on, folks get killed and we have to accept it and get on with things. Look on the bright side, love, your young man survived. They've taken him to Ely, it's a bleedin' long way from here, thirty-five miles I reckon. I've asked around and Eddie is happy to take you on the back of his motor bike.'

Hannah wasn't sure she wanted to go. How could she face Jack knowing she was protecting a German? This man wasn't personally involved but as far as everyone else was concerned he was a murdering, evil Luftwaffe pilot. She shuddered. If anyone realised he was still alive there would be a witch hunt. Captain Turner would be positively encouraged to execute the injured man. She had no choice, she must continue to protect Flt Lt Schumann, risk her freedom by taking him food and water whenever she could.

Joan was waiting for her answer. 'It's a nice thought, Joan, but I can't ride pillion when I only have one arm to hold on with. I'm sure I can get to Ely. I can catch the bus from Debfield and then get a train from Saffron Walden.'

'I'd forgotten about your arm, ducks, probably best you don't go with Eddie. There's a bus tomorrow morning at eight o'clock, why don't you get that one? I reckon you could catch a train to Ely from there. It might take you all day, you'll have to take an overnight bag, find a B&B to stop in.'

Hannah was torn. If she was away for two days the German would have nothing to eat and he'd run out of water by morning. If she got up at dawn she could take provisions and still be ready to catch the bus. 'I will go tomorrow, Joan.'

'Good idea, your young man won't be going anywhere for a week at least. Now, drink your tea then go and have a bit of a lie down, you don't look at all well.'

Hannah flung herself on her bed. She hugged her knees as she used to do when little. She couldn't abandon her patient; he had no one else to look out for him. He might be an enemy, but he was just an ordinary man caught up in a horrible war.

Jack was in hospital, *he* was in no danger. She scarcely knew him but everyone expected her to rush to his bedside. She'd agreed to be his special girl and he'd want her to come.

He'd be devastated by the deaths of his closest friends. She couldn't leave him to suffer on his own.

Scalding tears trickled down her cheeks. Why was she crying? Was it for Jack's crew, the injured German or Giles… missing, presumed dead, over France?

Chapter Seven

Hannah slept little that night, eventually abandoning the attempt and getting up. Feeling like a thief, she raided the pantry, filled up the flask and then collected a few more odds and ends that might come in useful at the barn.

A few desultory birds greeted the morning; the rooks were already fluttering about in the trees waiting to make their dramatic exit. She loved the way they muttered and mumbled as if discussing where they were going to go and feed that day before. Almost simultaneously thousands of the large black birds soared in to the sky. Despite her fatigue and bone deep misery, she paused to watch the spectacle. The birds wheeled and soared as if flying in formation like a gigantic swarm of bees and her spirits lifted a little. This had to be one of nature's miracles. How could one doubt the existence of a higher power when watching something so awe-inspiring?

She pedalled through the village in the dark but she was a dab hand at this bicycle lark now, even with a haversack and bulging basket she rarely wobbled.

This time she didn't creep up to the barn; she'd checked every few hundred yards no one was about in the fields. She propped her bike against the wall and started to unload the basket. A slight sound made her hair stand on end.

'Good morning, Fraulein, I did not expect to see you again. You must not continue to risk your safety on my account.' She turned her pulse slowing.

'You look a lot better. You shouldn't be out here in case anyone goes past. I think I'd better bring my cycle inside just in case.' To her surprise he removed the handlebars from her grip and wheeled it in himself. 'I had to come, things have changed; I'll explain what's happened.'

He propped the bike up before returning to the door and closing it. 'As you can see, Fraulein, I have not been idle in your absence.'

She glanced around. 'My word, if I didn't know you were living here I'd think this place had been deserted for years.'

His face was a white blob in the gloom. 'Do you have a torch with you?'

She rummaged in her pocket and tossed it over, he caught it one-handed. 'I can't leave it with you, I'm sorry, I've only got the one.'

'I have no wish to deprive you of its use. Look, I have hidden everything beneath that pile of corrugated iron. I dug the hole yesterday and placed everything in when I heard you approaching. I am ready for when they come to arrest me.'

'That's the problem—I can't tell them where you are even in a roundabout way.'

Over breakfast she explained what had happened reassured that he was horrified by the behaviour of his compatriots. 'So you see, Flt Lt Schumann, I'll have to hide you. I think if you were found today they might shoot you.'

'It is a sad world we are living in, Fraulein Hannah. This morning I am ashamed to be a German. My father died in the First World War. That was a pointless exercise but at least it didn't involve the civilian population.'

The sun shone through the holes in the peg tiles making it light enough to see. She was shocked to see tears on his cheeks. 'I have to go to Ely this afternoon; it would look odd if I didn't. I've brought food and some extra sacks. You'll be safe here for a couple of days. Everyone thinks all three of you died; I just hope it stays that way.'

'My head is healing well, if you bring scissors you can remove the stitches next time you come. When I am captured no one will know I have been assisted.'

'I'm hoping, once the funerals are over, people will forget about it. I've been thinking what we should do; you must take my bicycle and cycle as far away as you can then hand yourself in somewhere nobody knows about Pete and Dave.'

He reached out as if to touch her hand but changed his mind. 'I cannot take your bicycle. When I go I shall walk. You have done more than enough, I owe you my life.'

She scrambled to her feet embarrassed by his thanks. 'I've got to get a move on, I have to be back before my landlady misses me. I won't be here for three days. Take care of yourself. I know you're not a bad person any more than my boyfriend is.'

Debfield was still sleeping when she returned. She put her bicycle in the shed, grabbed a bucket and ran to the standpipe. The kitchen was empty, thank goodness - by the time Joan appeared she would have done her usual chores and her dawn ride would never be discovered.

Her gumboots were in the shed and her slacks had no tell-tale signs of her trek through the fields. Joan was there when Hannah pulled open the stairs door.

'Don't come up, ducks, bad luck to cross you know. You ready to leave?'

'Almost, I just have to get my bag and then I can go. I expect I'll have a lot of standing about to do. Do you have any idea where the RAF hospital is in Ely?'

'Not the foggiest, someone will tell you. Get a taxi from the station, but best sort your B&B before you go to the hospital. It gets dark early nowadays.'

A taxi was out of the question, she barely had enough money to pay for the accommodation as well as the train fare. Everyone thought she was well off but she had less money than either Betty or Ruby. She didn't know how she was going to manage if she couldn't work. She had several hundred pounds in a savings account but the book was elsewhere. Perhaps she'd have time to find a branch of her bank and arrange to withdraw money without having the passbook.

She joined a queue of locals waiting for the bus and they greeted her like an old friend. They knew her even if *she* didn't recognize *them*.

By the time the ancient vehicle coughed its way to the bus stop she knew that Mrs Reynolds was plagued by bunions, her friend Aggie was going through the change and that at least two of the other women had lost sons or relatives at Dunkirk or in North Africa.

She escaped the ladies with the excuse that her train was about to depart. It had been harrowing listening to their comments about Pete and Dave and they knew she was on her way to visit Jack and sent their good wishes.

The station master informed her the next train was going to Cambridge and all she had to do was count the stations to be sure of getting off at Ely. As she tucked herself in to a corner seat Hannah realised she hadn't thought to ask how many stops it would be. Since station names had been removed every traveller must know exactly where to get off, or they might sail through the station. The journey was uneventful and she had no problems getting out at Ely.

Outside the station the road was busy. The guard's instructions were excellent and she arrived outside the hotel he'd suggested without getting lost. Fortunately there was an attic bedroom vacant and she took it. She washed her face, revelling in the luxury of running hot water. She would definitely use the bathroom before she left.

She handed her key in at the desk and set out for the hospital. Her stomach rumbled loudly. There was a small cafe doing a brisk trade with early diners and she decided to join the queue. For 1s 6d she got a tasty meat pie, two veg and mashed potato, followed by jam roly-poly and custard, all washed down with a large mug of extremely strong tea.

The time was a little after one o'clock. Visiting at Saffron Walden hospital was restricted to two hours during the afternoon and two hours after supper.

There was a large notice prominently displayed in the hospital reception area telling her visiting times were strictly adhered to, that only one visitor was allowed per patient and visitors were not allowed to smoke in the wards. She had almost two hours to kill. Her haversack was stuffed with cake and scones for the invalid and these would spoil if carted around the city. She approached a nurse carrying a clipboard.

'Excuse me, I've brought food gifts for a patient, Flt Lt Rhodes. He was admitted yesterday with concussion and a shoulder injury. Would it be possible for me to leave them somewhere until visiting time?'

The young woman smiled. 'Here, I'll take them; I'm on duty in Ward 3. That's where he is. Who shall I tell him is here?'

'Tell him Hannah's here.' She handed over her haversack and the nurse vanished through double doors in to the bowels of the building.

Hannah decided to walk to the cathedral; she needed all the help she could get to sort out her muddled life. In less than a week she'd broken her arm, become embroiled in treasonable activity, and was the girlfriend of an injured RAF pilot.

*

'Time for your medication, Flt Lt Rhodes, and I've good news.'

Jack opened his eyes, remembering not to turn his head too quickly. He didn't have the energy to ask.

'Your young lady has come to see you, she asked me to bring you these. She can't come in until three o'clock.' The girl placed a cake tin on the bedside table then waited for him to hold out his hand for the painkillers and glass of water.

He had no appetite. The concussion had made him vomit several times during the night; all he wanted at the moment was water. Hannah had come all this way—that was kind of her considering they were only friends. He closed his eyes, willing himself to picture her face instead of those of his crew.

He drifted off to sleep and when he woke the ward lights were on and the blackout curtains drawn. The sound of voices other than those of the nurses meant it must be visiting time.

'At last, I thought you were going to sleep right through. I've had two cups of tea and a slice of your cake; it's delicious by the way.'

'Hannah, God, I'm sorry. You should have woken me—you've come all this way...'

'Don't worry about it. I'm just relieved you don't look as bad as I feared.' There were tears in her eyes as she leant forward. 'I can't tell you how sorry I am about Pete and Dave, I liked them both, the whole village is in shock.'

Unexpectedly grief overwhelmed him, tears dripped down his cheeks and he couldn't stop them. She moved to the bed and cradled him in her arms, rocking him, stroking his head gently as if he were a child. This was what he needed, he'd not been held since his mother died when he was eight years old.

'Shush, Jack, it's all right, you'll feel better letting it go. Don't blame yourself, no one else does. I know it's hard to accept but hundreds of men die every day, it's something we have to live with.'

She gave him a handkerchief; he wiped his eyes and blew his nose vigorously forgetting about his injured head. For a moment his vision blurred and he thought he was going to be sick over her.

'Keep still, the nurse said if you moved too quickly you'd feel nauseous.'

'Crickey! What must you think of me? First I blub all over you and then ...'

Her laugh cleared the last of his grief. He could cope without his friends if he had her to talk to. 'Hannah, are you staying tonight? Did you get a lift here or come by train?'

'Train, I'm staying at The Lamb. I hope there'll be a train back tomorrow as it's Saturday.'

Just having her sit beside him holding his hand was better than any medicine. Had things changed between them or was he imagining it?

*

Jack was clinging on to her like a lifeline; she didn't like to pull away. Good grief! She was holding hands and actually enjoying the sensation. He was a dear boy, nothing like ... she wouldn't even say his name in her mind. 'Do you know when you're going to be discharged? Are you going to convalesce with your family?'

'I'm an orphan and my two older sisters live in Cornwall.' His brow furrowed and his fingers tensed. 'I was thinking... would you mind if I came to stay in the pub with you? I can't think of anywhere else to go and Joan has rooms to let.'

She tried to hide her dismay, but failed. He removed his hand and looked hurt. She couldn't explain why she didn't want him there and didn't want him to think she was rejecting him. He was right - Joan was the right person to look after him. 'I'm so sorry; I think there's something I need to tell you.' His eyes narrowed and he waited without comment for her to continue. 'You've noticed I don't like to be touched - it's not you - it's any man.' She wasn't sure she could go on. He was staring at her as if he already despised her.

'Go on, sweetheart, I can guess what you're trying to tell me. Some bastard hurt you, didn't he?'

Her voice was little more than a whisper. 'I was engaged to him. It was my fault, I didn't even like him but my family pushed me in to it. I wouldn't have done it but Giles was missing…When I told him I didn't love him, wanted to end it, he … he raped me.' There, she'd said it. She couldn't look at him.

His warm fingers gently cupped her chin and turned her face towards him. 'You poor darling, no wonder you're nervous around me. Thank you for telling me; I won't do anything to upset you.' His voice hardened, he looked and sounded tough and frightening. 'If I ever get hold of him, Hannah, I'll break his neck after I've given him a damn good kicking.'

'You don't mind? You still want to go out with me?'

He reclaimed her hands. 'Of course I mind, but for your sake, not mine. I'll take care of you in future, nothing bad will happen to you whilst I'm around.'

That terrible afternoon no longer mattered. She'd found Jack and he didn't care. He wanted to protect her and keep her safe. Impulsively she kissed his cheek, his smile told her she'd done exactly the right thing.

Too soon the bell was rung and she had to go. She turned and waved at the door. He was sitting up looking ten times better than he had when she came in.

She almost skipped through the hushed corridors. She hesitated on the steps; things looked different in the dark. She shivered and her happiness shrivelled. How was she going to take care of her pilot when Jack was staying at the pub?

Chapter Eight

The bus for Debfield left Saffron Walden on time. Hannah squeezed in beside a stout lady with an extremely smelly baby on her lap. With luck she should be back at the pub before eleven o'clock.

'You been away for the night then? Got a young man then?' The stout lady nodded encouragingly expecting Hannah to reply. 'Been in the wars then? Broken your arm and that?'

'I broke my arm the other week falling over something.'

'You won't have heard then? Been a right to do hasn't there? Found out that German pilot what shot down our boys the other night wasn't burnt in his plane. What do you think of that then?'

The bus lurched to a halt in order to disgorge some of its passengers giving Hannah a few moments to recover from her shock. The smelly baby gave her a gummy grin and reached out a sticky finger. The baby's mother moved the infant away and he howled in protest. Hannah was relieved this gave her an opportunity to change seats without appearing impolite. 'I'm sorry; there are spare seats on the other side of the bus, if I move he'll soon forget about me.'

She stared out of the window making sure no one else attempted to engage her in conversation. She had to warn

Herr Schumann. If they were searching a barn would be the first place they'd look. He must move … but where to?

When she disembarked outside the village hall she was no nearer a solution and was on the verge of panic. If … *when* he was found no one would stop Captain Turner shooting him. She couldn't let this happen; she would do everything she could to protect him until he escaped. Jack was in hospital so this gave her some time before he was living under the same roof. Once he was there it would be impossible to sneak out without him being aware of it. Tears prickled behind her eyelids; he would never forgive her if he found out.

Joan was busy in the kitchen when Hannah went in. 'Welcome back, ducks …' she turned from the bowl where she was peeling potatoes. 'How's your young man?'

'Jack's fine. He wants to come here for a few days. I hope that's all right.'

'It'll be grand having a man about the place again. Will he be fit enough to lift a barrel?'

'Not initially - his shoulder's injured but he'll be able to help in other ways.' Hannah hugged Joan. 'I'll put my things away, have a quick wash, and cycle over to Pond Farm to tell Betty and Ruby what happened.'

'I'm not sure you should be gallivanting about the countryside at the moment. I don't suppose you heard the German's on the loose?'

'A lady on the bus told me. With the entire home guard and constabulary in the fields I'll be safer than ever.'

'Very likely! You were out the morning of the crash and came to no harm. A pity he didn't burn to death in the plane like everybody thought. He doesn't deserve to be alive after what he did to our boys You run along, I'll pack you something to eat and make your flask, it's a long way to cycle with nothing to eat at the end of it.'

'How did they know he wasn't dead?'

'A farmhand found a German flying helmet in a ditch. It didn't get there by itself, now did it?'

*

'Right, young man, you've made a remarkable recovery. I'd no intention of releasing you until next week but I'll reluctantly sign your discharge papers.' The doctor frowned. 'As your squadron leader's here to drive you and you've promised to take it easy for the next few days, I suppose you'll come to no harm.'

Jack was dressed. When Johnny arrived at visiting time with a spare uniform he was delighted. His leather flying jacket was blood-stained but wearable. 'Thanks, Doc, there are blokes who need the bed more than I do. I won't return to duty until the medic gives me the all clear. He can take out the stitches as well '

He wanted to be with Hannah. He loved her and was going to find it difficult not being able to show how much, but was prepared to wait as long as it took.

Johnny was outside the ward. 'I'm not convinced I should be helping you, old man, but won't stand between a man and his beloved. I've got the old boneshaker outside, hope it doesn't make your shoulder open up.'

'As long as you take it steady round the corners, I'll be fine. It'll be like a holiday staying in Debden.' No need to say being on the base would be unbearable without Pete and Dave.

The fresh air almost knocked him flat, he wasn't as fit as he'd insisted but was damned if he was going back now he'd got this far. A bony arm gripped his waist and steadied him. 'The car's right here, you'll be fine once you're in.'

His squadron leader drove an open topped sporty vehicle; Jack couldn't have got in a normal car. He slumped against the seat gritting his teeth waiting for the pain and dizziness to subside. A blanket was tucked round his legs as if he was a geriatric passenger. He didn't complain; it felt damn cold after the fug of the hospital.

He remembered little of the journey, dozed most of the way and when the car pulled up at The White Hart he felt better. 'Thanks for bringing me, Johnny, much appreciated. Not quite ready to come back, couldn't face the chaps at the moment. What's the time, do you know?'

'Nearly two o'clock. I have to get back, old fellow, a big op on tonight. The show must go on, and all that. I'll let them know you're here—don't expect you want to see anyone today.'

Jack braced himself and managed to get out of the car without aggravating his shoulder. The manoeuvre allowed him to control his grief before answering. Once upright, his jacket draped over his damaged shoulder, he nodded. 'Thanks again, for everything. Give me a couple of days and I'll be fighting fit.' He shook his head as Johnny started to prise himself out. 'Stay where you are, I can manage my kit-bag with my good hand. Send my regards to the lads - good luck tonight.'

His sadness lifted a little as he approached the kitchen door. He couldn't wait to see Hannah. Was she going to be pleased by his unexpected arrival?

Joan opened the door and slopped a bucket of dirty water over his boots. 'Jack! What are you doing here? Hannah said you weren't coming until next week.'

'I persuaded them they needed the bed more than they needed me. Is it all right for me to stay here until I can go back?'

She put the bucket down outside the door and nodded vigorously. Her eyes were brimming, he hoped she didn't set him off again. 'Of course it is, come along in. Sit down before you fall down. It won't take me a minute to make up a bed and light the fire, I've just made a pot of tea, help yourself.'

'Where's Hannah? She's the reason I've arrived early.'

'Heavens! She's not here; she's gone over to Pond Farm to see her friends and taken lunch with her. She'll be back before dark, plenty of time for you to get yourself settled in by then.'

*

Hannah cycled directly to the field that led to the barn. She prayed Joan wouldn't ask her anything about Pond Farm. With her hat pulled low to conceal her tell-tale hair she hoped no one would recognize her. If they spotted her from a distance she could be any land girl cycling to work. Occasionally she heard voices and once the roar of a motorbike almost sent her wobbling in to the ditch, but nobody came within hailing distance.

Her arm made it difficult to steer. Several times she almost came to grief, her long legs saving her from disaster. She stopped and rammed the bike in to the overgrown shrubbery that bordered the ditch and transferred everything from the front basket in to her haversack.

Now was not the time for casual strolling, she couldn't afford to be seen anywhere near the barn. The ditch was the obvious place to walk but today she took a different route. This meant another half an hour of brisk walking so she could approach from the front. If anyone had been there she'd have sufficient warning before she was seen.

Crouching as close to the hedge as she could she made her way around the huge meadow. Her fingers and feet were numb long before she could see the small stand of oak trees that blocked light from the barn.

She was on the far side of the thick hawthorns that made up the majority of the hedge; with luck this would hide her.

She paused, convinced the barn was either unoccupied or Herr Schumann was alone. She daren't emerge without checking; there might be someone waiting in ambush for the person who'd treacherously assisted the enemy.

She approached nervously; she would push the spiky branches apart and peer through. Her gloves were thick and with her jumper and coat covering her arms she should avoid getting scratched.

Carefully parting the black twigs with her cast, she looked through. Thank God! The broken door was just as she had left it, no sign of booted feet or army vehicle wheels anywhere in the grass surrounding the small barn. She smoothed back the twigs leaving the hedge undamaged. He was safe, but for how much longer?

She ran the twenty yards calling as she did so. She didn't want a repeat performance of a gun pointing at her heart. The rickety door swung open and he greeted her with a formal click of the heels and a half bow. He looked quite different. How tall he was, half a head bigger than her at least. Apart from his beard he looked quite smart.

'Good afternoon, Fraulein, I did not expect to see you until tomorrow. However, I am most relieved you have come.'

'Inside, quickly, we have no time to lose. They know that you didn't die in the fire and the whole neighbourhood's out searching for you. You have to leave straightaway.'

It took a few seconds for her eyes to adjust to the gloom and she stared in astonishment. The barn looked as if no one had been there for years. He had been waiting for her; he already knew what was going on.

'I am ready. I have not been spending all my time inside. I have been taking note of what is transpiring in the countryside. My ribs are healing well and I was able to ascend one of the trees. From my vantage point I saw the search begin.'

'No one would know you'd been here.' She'd no idea how to get him to safety. He was quite obviously a German pilot. Why hadn't she brought him something to wear? The sacks - he could disguise himself with those then he would be mistaken for a farm labourer especially if he walked with a stoop.

'The sacks?'

He pointed to a neat bundle tucked behind the door. 'I have all of them here and the other necessities that you were kind enough to bring me. What had you in mind, Fraulein?'

'Rip two of them apart, make holes for your head and arms then the other goes on top. Use this string to fasten it. If you cut a stick from the hedge you'll look like a farm worker, especially if you're with me.'

His nostrils pinched and she thought he would refuse. Then he nodded and walked stiffly to his parcel. Between them they constructed a decent disguise. He was disgusted he had to wear a sack over his blood-stained uniform. She had no sympathy, this was no time for pride, his existence depended on the sacks.

'Goodness, if I didn't know it was you, Herr Schumann, I'd not recognize you. We've got a couple of hours before dark. I'll find you somewhere safe to hide before then.'

'I have no wish to further endanger you. I must make my own way now; if I am apprehended, then so be it.'

'I wouldn't dream of it; on your own you'd be checked by patrols but travelling together we should be ignored. The area around Debfield and your crash site has been searched already, so it makes sense of you to go somewhere they've looked.'

He smiled, seeming years younger and less austere. 'You are an intelligent young lady; I believe you have an excellent idea. Do you have anywhere particular in mind?'

'I do - there's a derelict cottage on the outskirts of the village, they'll have gone over that. It's perfect. I can't come out in daylight again as my landlady's having an extra lodger.'

She held her breath waiting for him to ask who the lodger was. He would never agree to hide in the cottage if he knew the best friend of the murdered men was staying nearby.

All she had to do was walk him through the countryside in broad daylight, through the village and in to the cottage without being seen. What was she thinking? They would be spotted immediately—there must be another way to do this.

'If you will allow me to make a suggestion, Fraulein Hannah, it might well be best for me to hide outside the populated area until dark. You could come and fetch me to the cottage when everyone is asleep.'

She frowned—all very well for him, but how was she going to get out of the house in the middle of the night without Joan waking up? Shrugging off her fears she forced a smile. 'You're right, it's madness to go through the village. There's a hollow oak tree about a mile from Debfield, all the children know about it, so it's bound to have been searched. You can wait there.'

They walked openly along the edge of fields, he bending over his stick, she wheeling her bicycle. Twice she feared they'd be seen when a lorry full of soldiers thundered past on the other side of the hedge. It had taken too long to reach the oak; it would be dark in less than twenty minutes.

'In here, Flight Lieutenant, you can sit on your bundle and eat your food. I can't promise when I'll be back. My landlady goes to bed late. I'll come before it's light.'

There was no time for further talk. He vanished in to the tree and she swung onto her bicycle and rode furiously for home. God knows what tale she would tell Joan. She threw her bike in to the shed, kicked off her boots and rammed her feet in to her brogues then dashed for the back door. This opened as she reached it. Her heart almost stopped. It wasn't Joan standing there—but Jack.

Chapter Nine

'Hannah, I've been out of my mind. Where the hell have you been?'

'Jack, what a lovely surprise; if I'd known you were coming today I wouldn't have stayed out so long.' She covered her alarm by turning her back and appearing to struggle with her jacket. What should she say?

'God, I'm sorry. It's none of my damn business. I'm making a complete mess of this - I discharged myself especially to come and see you.'

He sounded so wretched and none of this was his fault. She turned and put her good arm around his neck drawing his head closer. Stretching on tiptoes she brushed her lips against his finding it unexpectedly pleasurable.

Her kiss distracted him. His arm encircled her waist and he gently covered her mouth with his. She stiffened. He paused, not increasing the pressure. Her momentary panic evaporated under the heat of something she didn't recognize.

'My word, you didn't waste any time, young man. Let the poor girl close the door, all the warmth's escaping.'

Joan's laughing comment had the same effect as a bucket of cold water and Hannah leapt back her face scarlet. She glanced at Jack and he was equally embarrassed. He pulled a face and winked. An irresistible urge to giggle made her look away.

He recovered his *sang froid* and laughed. 'Sorry, Joan.'

Reaching behind Hannah he latched the back door leaving her to escape to her bedroom before he could ask her any more awkward questions about where she'd been until dark. She barely had time to remove her shoes and put on her slippers when she heard Joan shout. She ran to the top of the stairs. 'What's the matter, Joan?'

'It's your Jack, he's come over all peculiar. He should never have left hospital; we have to get him in bed right now.'

Hannah almost fell down the stairs and burst in to the kitchen to see him slumped in a chair. His eyes were closed, sweat beading on his forehead. 'Jack, you have to go to bed. Can you stand if we help you?'

His eyes opened but they were unfocused, then he pulled himself together and smiled apologetically. 'Sorry, think I've overdone it. If I can lean on your shoulder, Hannah, I can just about stagger up.'

Between them they negotiated the narrow passage and got him in the room Joan had prepared. This was opposite Hannah's; she would be able to hear if he called out during the night.

'Do you want help to get undressed, Jack?'

He gripped onto the iron bedstead and shook his head. 'No, I can manage. You could give me a hand with my boots, when I put my head down it feels as though it's going to fall off.'

By the end he was almost unconscious. Joan removed his uniform and put him under the covers. 'Best we leave his long johns, don't want to embarrass the boy. He's got a po under the bed, and nice jug of water and I found that bottle of aspirin as well.'

Hannah straightened the sheets. His skin was burning; she didn't like the look off him at all. 'I'm going to cycle to the base and fetch Doctor Donnelly. I do wish Jack hadn't left hospital, he's made himself ill because of me.'

'It was his decision. Nothing to do with you, if he's made himself worse then it's his own fault. Don't worry - he's got a temperature – a bit of sponge down with tepid water and he'll be right as ninepence.'

'He doesn't need a doctor?'

'No point in making a fuss, Jack would hate it. You sit by his bedside and cool him off with this flannel. If he's no better in a couple of hours we can send for the doctor then. I expect there'll be a few boys in tonight, one of them can fetch him.'

Joan wasn't bothered by Jack's collapse. Hannah squeezed the flannel and dampened his face, the cloth came away almost dry. Perhaps if she opened the window, as well as removing the blanket, he would cool down more quickly. After an hour of this his temperature had reduced, his breathing was regular and the hectic flush along his cheek-bones had faded.

Several times she'd spooned water between his lips and the jug was empty. Was he well enough to leave whilst she went down to refill it? She rested her hand on his forehead and to her surprise his eyes opened.

'Sorry about all this, sweetheart, felt a bit groggy earlier. I'm okay now.'

'Oh, Jack, I'm so glad you've woken up – you had a rotten temperature. It's gone down now.'

She dropped beside him on the bed. 'Is there anything you need? I've going downstairs for more water.'

His grin was a trifle lopsided. 'Blow the water – what about half a pint of bitter instead?'

He was definitely on the mend. 'No – certainly not. I could bring a cup of tea?'

'Lovely. I could eat a sandwich if there's one going. Do you think you could close the window, it's like an ice house in here?'

Hannah hadn't noticed the cold until he mentioned it. 'Do you want me to light the fire?' She slammed the window and latched it, not an easy task when muffled behind the heavy blackout curtains.

'A couple of blankets will be fine, I don't mind the cold.'

Leaving him snugly tucked in she took a candle and groped her way down to the kitchen. She could hear Joan moving about in the bar. She looked at the clock on the shelf and saw it was almost opening time. Once the kettle was over the flames she went to speak to Joan. Jack wasn't the only one who needed a sandwich.

Joan was wiping her hands after lighting the fire in the public bar. 'You look more cheerful, ducks, your young man a bit better?'

'He is; demanding a cup of tea and sandwiches. Is it all right to make us something to eat? We both missed our tea tonight.'

'There's some tasty soup just waiting to be heated and I baked this morning so the bread's lovely and fresh. Help yourself. Jack's a paying guest so he can have whatever he wants.' Joan grinned. 'And so can you, ducks, you know that.'

Carrying a laden tray was going to be tricky with only one good arm. Hannah decided to make two journeys - take the sandwiches up on a plate and then come back for the mugs of tea. She could still clutch a candlestick with the fingers protruding from her plaster cast. Jack greeted her as if she had been gone for hours not minutes.

'At last! I heard Joan unbolting the door. The thought of all that beer downstairs and me up here as dry as a desert is making me miserable.'

She put the plate of sandwiches on the bedside table. 'I'm going back for the tea, there's cheese and pickle and spam and mustard, help yourself.'

As she left the room she heard Betty's voice outside and the rattle of bicycle wheels. Her heart skipped; she must speak to her before Joan said anything. She flew down the stairs and out of the back door in her slippers arriving at the side of the pub just as Betty, Ruby and Daphne dismounted.

'Betty, I need to speak to you, it's urgent.'

'Hello, Hannah, what you doing out here without your coat, it's perishing?' Betty dumped her bike against the wall and came over, the pinprick of light from her torch wavered across Hannah's face.

'Please, if Joan says anything tell her I was with you this afternoon. Jack's upstairs, I've got to get back, but I'll come in the bar as soon as I've eaten my sandwich and explain.'

'Fair enough, we've got plenty to tell you as well. It was a right laugh at the farm today.' Betty turned to the other two. 'Come along, ladies, I could do with a nice port and lemon.'

Hannah's slippers were too wet and dirty to wear inside, she'd tell Joan she went outside and forgot to change. More lies - and what was she going to tell the girls to explain where she'd been?

She dumped her slippers in the scullery. Snatching up the tea she headed for the stairs, this time she'd left a candle burning in the narrow passageway so she could see her way to Jack's room.

'Sorry, I'd forgotten to put the bread in the bread bin. We're plagued with mice, I'm going to get a cat for Joan. There are several on the farm no one would miss.' She handed him a mug of tea and he took several noisy gulps.

'I've eaten one of each; you have what you want and I'll finish the rest.'

Her appetite had gone, but she needed to force something down or she'd feel faint later on. She mumbled her way through a cheese and pickle sandwich, the bread was fresh and turned to a lump in her mouth. She managed to wash it down with a swallow of tea.

The sound of voices in the bar gave her an excuse to leave before he began to ask awkward questions. She was praying his sudden collapse had blotted out the memory of her absence.

'I can hear Betty and the girls downstairs. Do you mind if I go down and have a chat to them? They'll want to know how you are.' She brushed the crumbs from her lap and then stared at them in dismay. 'How stupid! I'll have to get the dustpan and brush, you can hear the mice running about in the roof ...' she shivered dramatically. 'At least I hope they're mice. Joan doesn't like food upstairs in the normal way. Would you like some more tea?'

He drained the mug and held it out, his eyes dancing with amusement. 'You're a walking disaster area, my love. What happened to your slippers? I suppose you had some accident with them as well?'

She grinned. 'I went outside in them - big mistake. Good thing I've got thick socks on. I'll not be a minute; don't die of thirst whilst I'm gone.'

By the time she'd swept up all the debris from the impromptu supper, washed up the dirty plates and mugs and returned them to the dresser, there was a fair bit of noise from the bar. She'd settle Jack with a fresh jug of drinking water and promise to look in on him before she went to bed.

'Douse the candles, love, I'm ready for a kip.'

'Sleep well. I'll be along later to check on you.'

She hesitated in the doorway wondering whether she should kiss him goodnight but he was already asleep.

She couldn't put it off any longer. Betty would be coming through to find her if she didn't go. The usual fug of smoke and damp clothing hung over the public bar; the saloon was empty, the fire not even lit. She was greeted by several of the customers, but nodded and hurried to join her friends at a table in the corner.

'Sorry I've been so long, he's fallen asleep now. Is that the doctor by the window?'

'Yes, he wants to talk to you before he leaves, he thinks Jack was barmy coming out of hospital so soon.' Betty pulled out a chair and pointed to a glass of ginger beer. 'We got you this, didn't think you wanted anything alcoholic.'

Hannah took as long as she could to sip her drink and greet each of the girls in turn. They were waiting expectantly to hear why they'd had to cover for her. 'I told Jack about... well you know what and needed time to think about things on my own.'

Ruby stretched across the table and squeezed Hannah's hand. 'Don't worry, we'll not tell anyone.'

The other two nodded agreement. 'Thank you, if you don't mind I'd rather not talk about it anymore. Betty, you said you had something funny to tell me? I need cheering up.'

When she heard Captain Turner had searched Pond Farm she thanked God Herr Schumann had moved before the home guard found the barn. 'From what you say, Betty, no one would mind if he killed the pilot. Surely that can't be right?' If she had announced she'd stolen the crown jewels she couldn't have had a more unfavourable reaction.

'How can you say that when the German gunned down Pete and Dave in cold blood? That Nazi doesn't deserve sympathy. I'm surprised at you, Hannah.' Daphne pursed her lips and shook her head.

Betty added her two pennyworths. 'Don't let Jack hear you, given half a chance he'd be out with a gun in his hand, looking for himself. Bleedin' heck, Hannah, what sort of a girlfriend are you?'

Scarlet faced Hannah tried to think of some way of explaining her remark. Fortunately Dr Donnelly chose that moment to wander over to speak to her.

'How is the dear boy? Joan said he had a fever earlier.'

'Excuse me, girls, I'll just have a quick word with the doc.'

She edged the medic to the far side of the room before answering 'He's fine now, Doctor Donnelly. He ate a couple of sandwiches and had two mugs of tea and fell asleep. I'll make sure he doesn't get up until you say he can.'

'Good girl, I'll come and change the dressing on his shoulder tomorrow.'

They arranged for him to come mid-morning. Hannah didn't re-join her friends. She didn't blame them for being upset with her; she'd feel the same in their position. If they knew *her* German was a civilised man, hadn't killed Pete and Dave, maybe then they would understand.

Upstairs was quiet; she pushed open Jack's door, he was breathing evenly. Relieved she wouldn't have to speak to him, she retreated to her bedroom. Whatever her motives, she was a traitor and was betraying Jack as well as her friends.

She was committed, couldn't back out, and as soon as Joan was asleep she had to get dressed and take Herr Schumann to the derelict cottage. She was going to give herself away. God knows what would happen when her treachery became known.

She daren't risk falling asleep so remained fully clothed and sat beside the dying fire waiting for the village to quieten. The remaining sandwiches were wrapped in greaseproof paper and the thermos was full. These were under her bed in case Joan popped her head in to say goodnight.

She didn't light a candle. Jack might wake and see the flicker under his door. She went down the treacherous staircase with only the pinprick of light from her torch. With every board that creaked she froze expecting to be discovered. She was shaking by the time she reached the back door and she still had to get through the village and guide Kurt to the cottage.

There was no moon. This would make it harder for her

but at least they were less likely to be seen. Her haversack bounced painfully on her hip as she jogged along the grassy verge to the small wood outside Debfield. An owl hooted, its mate replied, a dog fox barked in the distance. She blundered in to a milk churn sending it clattering. A dog barked and someone sleepily yelled at it to be quiet.

Her hands were trembling. She grabbed the handle of the churn and stood it upright then fled and reached the edge of the village before realizing she should have left the churn alone. The occupants thought a cat had knocked it over, finding it replaced might rouse their suspicions.

Should she go back? No, she'd do it on her return, the sooner she got Herr Schumann safely hidden the better.

Twenty yards from the tree there was the unmistakable sound of a car approaching at high speed. There was nowhere to hide. How could explain why she was outside in the middle of the night?

Chapter Ten

Hannah shuffled sideways and turned her face away from the approaching vehicle. The vehicle was almost on her. With a roar and a blast of engine fumes it shot past and disappeared in to the darkness. Her legs wobbled and she collapsed in the dirt waiting for the sickness to pass.

The car could be back at any moment. It might be looking for her, might be going to knock on the door at the pub and then Jack and Joan would discover she wasn't in her bedroom. She scrambled to her feet and ran straight to the hollow tree.

'Flight Lieutenant, quickly, I was almost caught just now.' He emerged from the tree a bulky parcel under its arm. 'We must be quiet, I've disturbed one dog tonight, I don't want to do it again or someone might come out to investigate.'

'My night vision is of the most excellent. Go ahead, Fraulein, I shall be able to keep with you without difficulty.' His hissed whisper echoed eerily around the dell.

She pointed her torch in the right direction and set off, when they reached the back of some cottages, she stopped. 'This is the worst bit – there are pigs in the back gardens, they'll make a dreadful racket.'

He gripped her shoulder to show he understood. The first three cottages were crossed but then she trod on a branch.

The noise was shockingly loud. He stumbled in to the back of her almost tipping her over. He grabbed her. She was rigid waiting for a dog to bark and alert their owners

Silence stretched, she relaxed. They were safe this time. Standing, warmed by his closeness, steadied her nerves. His heart beat slowly; night time manoeuvres didn't scare him. She moved and immediately his arms dropped. He'd been offering comfort in the darkness the way Jack would. Kurt Schumann was a good man, she was glad she was keeping him safe. He didn't deserve to die.

Once past the houses they moved quickly. The abandoned cottages had been searched twice according to Joan. The authorities shouldn't look there again, only a madman would hide in the village.

'Here we are, the back door's open. Keep off the path; it's covered with bits after the last storm.' The interior smelt damp and musty, the furious scuffling in the darkness meant there were rats or mice. 'I thought you could use the back bedroom, the roof's sound and it faces the fields. You won't be seen up there.'

They climbed the twisting stairs and reached the room. He was the first to break the silence.

'This is excellent; I can make myself warm and comfortable here.'

Hannah crossed to the window. 'Nail one of the sacks here at night then you can light a candle. You can't have a fire so you're going to be frightfully cold.'

'It will be far better than the barn. I shall be content in my new lodgings. Have you any idea when I can surrender without danger of being shot?'

'After the next sortie; planes are shot down most nights. People will have other things to talk about. The men that died won't be forgotten, but it will seem less awful when things get back to normal.'

Too much talking, she must return to the pub before she

was missed. She removed the flask and other items from her haversack. 'You need to drink the tea, I have to go. I expect you heard the car go past just earlier, I can't be found out here tonight.'

He took the thermos and gulped the hot liquid—he must have been parched. He screwed the stopper and top and handed it back. 'There, *danke*, most refreshing. Now, Fraulein Hannah, you go. Do not visit me again; I shall be perfectly safe up here.'

'I'm not going to let you starve. If anyone finds you they would soon work out someone's been helping you, so too late to worry about all that. My boyfriend's staying at the pub, he's the pilot of the plane ... it was *his* crew who were killed. He's ill, but once he's up I shan't be able to come.'

'*Gott in Himmel* - how can that be? For such a coincidence the hand of Providence must surely be upon us. I have no wish to come between you and your young man. I shall hand myself in immediately.'

'Please, don't. We've come this far, let me get you away safely.'

'I could not live if I had your incarceration upon my conscience.'

He was determined to do the right thing. 'Promise me not to do anything rash. When I bring a bike you can escape from Debfield.'

'Very well, I shall do nothing. Take care; do not come if there is the slightest danger of you being apprehended. Helping the enemy in Germany would mean being executed without trial.'

The hair on the back of her neck prickled. Would it be any different in England? 'I have to go, I don't know how you're going to manage with… well you know what. Whatever you do, don't go outside to do it.'

His soft laughter lightened the mood. '*Auf wiedsehen*, my brave young lady.'

Her return journey was equally hazardous. Twice she crouched behind a hedge waiting for a dog to stop barking. She removed her gumboots and the empty haversack and left them beside her bicycle in the shed then slipped on her brogues without tying them. If Joan or Jack heard her on the stairs she'd tell them she'd been outside to the privy, that her stomach was upset. As long as they didn't see she was dressed she'd be okay.

The bolts slid back noiselessly. She hung her jacket on the peg in the scullery and crept in to the kitchen. Should she make herself a bottle? Her hands and toes were numb - was it worth the risk of discovery in order to be warm? The range was hot enough to warm the kettle. She left it on while she stole through the house to her bedroom. The room was freezing but silly to light the fire when she was going to bed.

She removed her clothes and pulled on a flannelette nightdress and cardigan. She couldn't push her plaster cast in to the sleeve of her dressing gown. Suitably dressed for someone who'd just tumbled out of bed, she retraced her steps. The kettle was hissing, she made herself a cup of tea and filled her hot water bottle.

She was passing Jack's room when he called out.' Hannah, is that you creeping about out there? What are you doing up in the middle of the night?'

She nudged his door with her shoulder. 'I needed to go outside, if you must know, and I'm cold and made another bottle and a cup of tea.' She held up the candlestick; he was swinging his legs out of bed intending to get up.

'Is there any more tea in that pot? I'm going to follow your example, I know there's a gazunder but I'm well enough to brave the elements.' He chuckled. 'Someone would have to empty it tomorrow morning. Guess whose job that would be?'

'Don't go anywhere until I get back. I'll put my bottle in

the bed and then come with you. Don't argue, Flight Lieutenant Rhodes, you can't go otherwise.'

Hannah reached her bedroom without dropping anything. She leant against the wall her knees trembling. What
if she hadn't changed? What if he'd woken up five minutes
earlier? Sweat trickled between her shoulder blades - if
this deception continued she would be in pieces. Heaven
knows how the young women who parachuted in to France
managed when faced with Gestapo. *She* couldn't cope when
it was Jack wanting to speak to her.

He was waiting, propped against the door frame of his
bedroom, his greatcoat over his shoulders and boots on his
bare feet. 'Aren't you bringing your tea back? We could drink
it together. I've missed you.'

She offered her shoulder for him to lean on, holding
her candlestick up in her good hand. 'I'm not an octopus;
something had to stay up here, didn't it?'

'Sorry, brain not engaged. I woke up in a fearful sweat, I
was dreaming about Pete and Dave.'

'I'm not surprised; it's going to take a while to get over
it. We can't walk side by side on the stairs. Can you brace
yourself with your good arm?'

'I'll lean my backside against the wall and hold on to the
banister with my good hand. If I slide down I should be safe
enough.' He nodded solemnly. 'However, I don't advise you
to walk in front of me.'

A deal of shuffling later he was in the kitchen. She
unbolted the back door and handed him the torch from
her cardigan pocket. 'Be careful, it's freezing and the flags
are slippery.' With a cheerful wave he set off down the short
path that led to the lavatory. She hovered anxiously inside
the kitchen until she heard him clumping back.

She opened the door just enough for him to slide through,
that way the lights could stay on. 'Your tea's made; I'll close
the range and bolt the door then carry it for you. We mustn't

stay here, we'll disturb Joan.'

Whilst he edged his way to his bedroom she put his tea on the side table. He looked pale and poorly, it would be several days before he could get up. She should have been concerned but was mainly relieved she had another night to herself. Would he think she was seeing another man? Better that than knowing the truth. It had been close tonight, she would be more careful tomorrow.

She was worried she wouldn't be awake to do her chores and was tempted to sit up and not climb in to her nice, warm bed. Her eyes drooped; she jerked awake, slopping tepid tea on the rag-rug. She'd be fit for nothing tomorrow if she didn't get some proper sleep.

The sound of the milk cart roused her. Even with black-outs drawn Hannah could see sunlight filtering in. She'd overslept. Why hadn't Joan called her? No time for a proper wash so she splashed her face with cold water, gave her teeth a cursory clean and pulled on yesterday's clothes. The curtains were open in the corridor. Jack's door was closed; she hesitated outside. Should she knock or go downstairs and apologise to Joan?

The decision was made for her when he shouted from downstairs. Good grief, he wasn't supposed to be up and about. 'Coming, sorry, I slept in. What are you doing up? Doctor Donnelly said you were to stay in bed for another three days.'

He certainly looked better; his cheeks had a healthy glow. He'd had a shave and managed to put his bad arm through his shirt and jacket sleeves. She felt unkempt. 'Joan said to leave you; you've had a rough old week in one way or another.'

She stared at him. 'Hardly - a broken arm is nothing compared to crash landing.'

His sweet smile did something funny to her insides. 'I've been getting in the way down here but I couldn't stay in bed. I promise I'll have a lie down later.'

An appetising smell wafted through from the kitchen and her stomach rumbled loudly much to his amusement. 'I know, very unladylike, but I didn't eat my sandwich last night. I hope there's plenty of toast, I'm absolutely starving.'

Instead of going ahead of her he stood to one side to let her pass. As she squeezed by his arms slid around her waist and drew her close. She was beginning to love this holding business.

'Sweetheart, I can't tell you what it means to me to be here. I can talk to you about it without seeming like a wet blanket. You understand what they meant to me, that they were my family.'

She twisted and stretched her good arm out to stroke his cheek. 'I'm your family now, I've got nobody else. I have to accept Giles might be dead and I'm not close to my father. I'll never go back.'

He placed his hand over hers moving it so he could kiss each fingertip in turn. A strange warmth slid along her limbs.

'Blimey, you two, it's not even eight o'clock and here you are canoodling in the corridor. I'd better move you to the other side of the building, Jack. I won't have hanky-panky under this roof, I can tell you.'

His face turned beetroot. He mumbled an apology Hannah smiled apologetically. 'Don't worry, Joan, I'm not that sort of girl and I trust Jack completely.'

Their landlady stood with her hands on her hips, her wraparound pinny quivering with indignation. 'That's all right then, but you'd be better off in the bedroom next to mine, young man. Hannah you can sort that out after break-fast.'

No more was said but there was a definite atmosphere in the kitchen. Joan kept giving them sidelong looks of dis-approval. Hannah wasn't a paying guest; she could be sent packing so would have to make sure she did nothing else to upset her landlady.

'Jack, can you fetch water whilst I sort out the rooms?'

'Good idea, I'm sure I can carry a bucket with my left hand. Is the nearest standpipe the one opposite the village hall?'

'Yes, I warn you it's probably busy, you're going to have people offering their sympathies.'

'I can deal with that, I've got to get on with things. In a couple of weeks I'll be flying again with a different crew. It won't help any of us if I'm still brooding.' He half smiled at her. 'I was intending to retrain as a fighter pilot and shoot down as many Luftwaffe as I could. Don't look like that, darling, I've come to my senses and accepted these things happen.'

'I'm not sure which is worse, flying a Hurricane or Spitfire, or being a bomber pilot. I'm sure both are equally dangerous; promise me you won't hurry back to the base until you're absolutely fit?'

He glanced nervously over his shoulder before taking her hands. 'I'm sorry, I can't promise that. I have to get back on duty ASAP. They don't have enough pilots and if we're going to win this war chaps like me can't sit about when they should be fighting.'

The changeover didn't take long; she just had to transfer the bedding to the room next to Joan's and remake the bed. Jack didn't have many personal belongings and he could move these himself. The fire hadn't been lit so she removed the newspaper, kindling and coal and carried this in the bucket and re-laid the fire.

This room was considerably smaller, it would be easier to keep warm than the other one. Also she'd be able to sneak out to see Herr Schumann without fear of being overheard. All she had to do now was make peace with Joan. The butcher's van called today, if she offered to do the queuing this morning that might do the trick.

Joan handed her the three ration books and two half crowns. 'A bit of stewing steak would be lovely, but I don't suppose he's got any. Get what you can, ducks, he's got an eye for a pretty girl. Give him one of your smiles and you'll get a pound of sausages from under the counter.'

'I need to go in to town later. I must get some money transferred so I can pay my way. I'm not doing nearly enough to compensate for board and lodging.'

'Don't be daft, ducks, take no notice of what I said. Seeing you two all lovey-dovey made me miss my old man. As long as you keep it clean, you have a cuddle whenever you feel like it.'

Chapter Eleven

The bar was heaving that night, air crew from the base poured in to drink the health of their lost comrades. It was Saturday night and nobody wanted to be sitting about moping. Hannah was too busy helping Joan to spend much time with her friends who had also cycled over. Jack joined his mates halfway through the evening; although he was quiet he didn't seem especially upset by all the fuss and attention he was getting.

By nine o'clock most of the locals had gone home, only Betty and the other land girls, plus personnel from the base, remained. Joan nodded to the group by the dart board.

'Go on, ducks, you've done more than enough. Take the weight off your feet, sit with your young man and your friends until closing time.'

Hannah didn't need telling twice, with a smiling thank you she carried her tray of dirty glasses out to the scullery, washed her hands in the basin and returned to the bar. Jack was waiting by the door.

'At last, I hate to see you working so hard, it can't be good for your broken arm. Joan's sent you a ginger beer, sit down and enjoy it.' He took her hand and led her over to the crowded table.

Ruby screeched a greeting. 'About blooming time, you look done in, I reckon you'd be better back with us than slaving away here in all this ciggie smoke.'

As usual there was a blue haze hanging halfway up the room. 'I know, and we can't even open the windows. I didn't expect to see any of you tonight, does old Boothroyd know you've escaped?'

'That's the funny thing, Mrs B came home in a right good mood and told us to pack up early and go and see you. What's that all about then?'

Hannah grinned. 'I met her in town and we had tea together, she's really very sweet, I've promised to come over and visit more often. I've also suggested she calls here whenever she's in the village doing her shopping.'

Jack nodded his approval. 'Good for you, she needs a friendly face or two to cheer her up. Did you manage to do what you wanted in town?'

'I did, eventually, I should get a letter confirming this on Monday.' She smiled across at her friends to include them in the conversation. 'I've been desperately short of money since I arrived at Pond Farm; I forgot to bring my bank book when I left in such a hurry. By the middle of next week I should be in funds again, I shall treat you all to a round or two next time you come in.'

Nobody suggested she play the piano, the mood was subdued but not unduly so. A couple of times Pete and Dave were mentioned, glasses were raised and for a second or two the group fell silent. Jack brought up the subject of the funeral.

'Are the burial arrangements in hand? I know Pete told me if he bought it he wanted to be buried in the cemetery at Cambridge.'

Another pilot, Bill Sanderson, nodded. 'That's what's happening, both of them are going to be buried with full honours on Monday. Wing-Co asked me to tell you but I didn't like to mention it. A car will collect you at seven o'clock, I don't suppose you have your dress uniform here, you'll need to come back and change.'

'You're right I don't, we need to give them a good send-off ...'

He was distressed so she quickly changed the subject. 'Joan says there's a *social* next Saturday at the village hall. I didn't like to tell her I'd no idea what that was.'

Later the discussion turned to cheerier subjects and they all agreed it would do them good to

attend the event which included a bit of dancing, party games for the children and card games for those that wanted them.

When time was called the RAF personnel were as raucous and jolly as they always were on a Saturday night. Whilst Jack helped Joan in the bar Hannah headed for the kitchen to put the milk on for their drinks. One thing about being in the country dairy products didn't seem to be in short supply.

'I'm going to take mine up, I'll leave you two lovebirds alone. Don't worry about getting up at the crack of dawn, Hannah love, it's Sunday. I expect you'll want to go to church the both of you.'

Fortunately Joan didn't wait for an answer. Jack raised his eyebrows. 'I'm not a regular attendee; we get church parade most Sundays and as a senior officer I'm expected to put in an appearance. The padre keeps it short, it's bloody cold in an aircraft hangar this time of the year. However, if you want to go tomorrow morning I'll be happy to come with you.'

The last thing she wanted was to dress up and be stared at by a congregation of accusing eyes. 'I'm pretty casual about going myself. I'm afraid I'm not totally convinced by the rhetoric. I believe in God, I think, but don't like organised religion.'

He shrugged apparently unbothered by her shocking admission. 'In which case we can spend a lazy morning together. I noticed there's a couple of board games tucked away in the bar, just the ticket. I'm a dab hand at ludo, draughts and snakes and ladders.'

'I have to do to my chores first, I promised to set some rat traps for Joan, I've not had the chance to do it yet.'

'I can hardly wait; I've always wanted to spend Sunday morning killing rodents. You're right, what she needs is a cat; why don't we see if we can get her one?'

'I mentioned it to Mrs Boothroyd this afternoon and she said I can come any time. Catching it is going to be difficult; they're fairly undomesticated. They live in the yard and most don't let you touch them.'

His chair moved and he rocked against the table making her swallow her cocoa too fast. He helpfully thumped on the back whilst she choked. 'Are you all right? Didn't mean to make you jump. So tomorrow we're going to do the rat traps and walk to Pond Farm and try and catch the cat?'

She mopped up the spilt drink from the table and scowled at him; he was unimpressed by her fierce expression. 'Why not do both? It doesn't take long to do the traps as I already know where the rat runs are. Can you ride a bicycle with your bad shoulder?'

He flexed his arm experimentally. 'I think so, I'll give it a go anyway. I don't have my bicycle here, is there one I can use?'

'I noticed a man's bike in the shed, it probably needs the tyres pumping up but it looked okay to me.' The clock on the mantelpiece struck eleven. 'I'm going up now. Don't forget your bottle, I've just filled it so it's piping hot.'

With hers tucked under her arm she led the way up. 'Goodnight, Jack, I won't wake you tomorrow morning, get up when you like. Joan said she's not going to open at lunchtime, she's almost run out of beer until the dray comes on Tuesday.'

In reply he bent his head and lightly brushed her lips with his own. She was beginning to enjoy this kissing lark. 'Goodnight, sweetheart, I can't believe it was only last Saturday we officially met. It's as though I've known you months, not days.'

'I feel the same. Doesn't everyone say that we must make the most of today as we don't know what the future holds.'

*

Jack preferred his new room; it reminded him of his childhood home when his mum had been alive. Things had been different after her death, his sisters had done their best but much of the time he'd gone to bed without supper and to school in unwashed clothes.

His dad never recovered and as the years passed he become more taciturn and withdrawn. If it hadn't been for Mr Frazer, his schoolmaster, things would have been quite different. Getting a full scholarship and a bursary to the posh school in the next town had changed his life. He smiled grimly. No doubt he would now be a private in the army like most of his junior school friends, not an officer in the elite service. It was bloody hard keeping up the pretence he was from a good home, many of the other blokes in the mess had attended public schools because their folks had enough money to pay for them, not because they were bright enough to get a scholarship.

Joan had put a match to the fire when she'd gone to bed and he was blissfully warm. He pulled back the slippery eiderdown and then the blankets and pushed the bottle between the sheets. He would become soft if he stayed here too long.

He wasn't ready to sleep; times like this he wished he smoked like most of the other chaps. He'd given it a go but it had made him feel sick and he didn't like the sour taste of tobacco in his throat. He'd got a couple of Raymond Chandler novels Doc had lent him, he'd get them out and give one a try.

He chose, *The Big Sleep*, thought the title appropriate for someone suffering from temporary insomnia. He was unused to having so much leisure time, even when he wasn't flying he was busy training new bods or involved in strategy meetings with the bigwigs. He stretched out on the bed, the warm lump of the bottle in the small of his back, and began to read.

He couldn't involve himself in the story. He kept thinking about his friends, how that German bastard had killed them in cold blood. Why hadn't the authorities tracked down the missing Nazi? Was a German sympathiser helping him? He had his revolver in his kit bag - tomorrow morning he'd start looking himself. Hannah could go to the farm on her own. He couldn't rest peacefully until he'd avenged his friends.

The cold woke him a couple of hours later. He sat up. Dammit, he needed a pee, he wasn't going to use the pot, he'd make the trek to the privy. Thank God he hadn't got in to his pyjamas.

Using his torch to guide him, his feet bare inside his unlaced boots, he shuffled to the back door. He reached out to unbolt it and was surprised to find it already open. Was Hannah out there? He waited a few minutes, when she didn't appear he became concerned. Perhaps she'd taken a tumble on the slippery flagstones; she was an accident waiting to happen.

A torch wasn't necessary, the moonlight bathed the path. There was no light flickering behind the privy door so she definitely wasn't in there. He'd been certain she'd pushed the bolts across before they'd gone to bed but he must have been mistaken. Never mind, he'd it done now.

*

The walk to the cottage was less eventful this time. Hannah kept to the road, knocked nothing over and disturbed no sleeping dogs. Kurt was waiting for her by the back door. He must have remarkable hearing as she'd been certain she'd been silent.

They didn't speak until safely upstairs. 'Good evening, Fraulein, you are a most welcome visitor. I have been eagerly anticipating the hot tea you bring me.'

'It's perishing in here, I've managed to bring three more sacks, they'll help a little.' He was mad not to wear them over his uniform, she wouldn't be so pernickety if she was stranded. 'The funeral's on Monday morning. I'm pretty sure after that things will settle down. I'll bring you a man's bike that night. I'll try and get to you earlier than this and then you must get as far away from here as you can and hand yourself in.'

'I cannot take a bicycle from you. Suspicion will immediately descend on your shoulders; it is too great a risk.'

'You've no choice. I'll make it look as though you've broken in and stolen it. I'm in far greater danger coming out here every night.' She immediately regretted her sharp words, the last thing she wanted was for him to rush off before Pete and Dave were buried.

'I understand perfectly. I have decided to surrender myself. I have no wish for you to return here again. When I have exhausted my supplies and become too cold and miserable to continue, I shall knock on the nearest cottage door.'

'My God, you mustn't do that. The only way we can both be safe is for you to do as I say. Wait until Monday night and then put as much distance between yourself and Debfield as you can.

'I suggest you ride south, towards Braintree. I think there might be another sortie tomorrow so that would be an ideal time for you to appear. Some of your pilots are bound to be shot down; with luck you'll be taken for one of them.'

His lips thinned, he didn't like being given orders. Then he smiled and offered his hand. 'I beg your pardon, please accept my apologies. I shall do as you request. Now, I am sure that you must wish to return to your bed as soon as possible. I shall drink your delicious tea and then you can leave.'

As she pushed the flask back in to the empty haversack he touched her arm. 'My dear, you must not come here tomorrow night. I can manage perfectly well until Monday without you putting yourself at unnecessary risk.'

She felt a rush of affection for this stranger, if only everybody knew what he was like there wouldn't be this witch-hunt going on. 'Thank you, if you're sure, it would make life a lot easier if I didn't have to come out again. I promise I'll bring food for your journey and more tea on Monday night. Keep safe, Kurt.'

He clicked his heels. 'I wish we had met in different circumstances, Hannah. I come originally from Bavaria, there the people are quite different. Not many of us support the Fuhrer, but unfortunately we are in the minority. If we wish to survive we must do as we are instructed.'

This was the first time the conversation had touched on his private life. War was horrid, making people like him do things they would never have considered before. She stretched up and kissed his unshaven cheek. 'Take care; it's Sunday tomorrow so hopefully everyone will be thinking holy thoughts and not looking for you.'

Not waiting for his reply she hurried out, the temperature had dropped by several degrees; it was still early November but cold enough for snow. Keeping to the shadows she retraced her steps and quickly slung her haversack in to the pannier on her bike. She was too tired to bother about that now, she'd tell Joan she'd forgotten to bring the flask in from the morning if she looked for it tomorrow. The end of her nose was icy, her toes and fingers numb, the sooner she was tucked up in her warm bed and clutching her hot water bottle the better.

Ignoring the rustling of the rats she crept to the back door and lifted the latch. It didn't open. Had the frost made it stick? She pulled harder, it didn't budge. The door was bolted. She was locked out. If she had to spend the rest of the night out here she would freeze to death.

Would it be possible to find somewhere warm at the back of the shed, cover herself with old sacks? No, how stupid, she'd taken all those to the cottage. She could go back there but she didn't fancy spending the night with Kurt. What about cycling to the farm? Betty and Ruby would take her in. She shivered - far too cold - and she didn't have a reasonable explanation for being locked out.

She wasn't going to knock Joan up, trying to explain to her and Jack would be even worse than talking to the girls. Then inspiration struck. The small window in the scullery had a broken catch, maybe she could wriggle in through there. The wooden frame flew open when she tugged. This was so high in the wall she needed a box to stand on. There must be something suitable in the junk heap at the back of the shed. She shone her torch in the darkness and spotted an old orange box. This would be perfect, not too heavy to move but rigid enough to support her weight.

After upending it under the window she scrambled up and pushed her head and shoulders through the gap, first waving her torch around to make sure she wasn't going to send a pile of dirty glasses smashing to the floor. She'd forgotten the old copper was directly under the window, the wooden lid was across the top so she could land on that without damaging herself or anything else.

With her arms outstretched she launched herself forwards praying she wouldn't get stuck half way. She had already removed her coat and dropped it in. By holding her breath somehow she got in without mishap. Apart from scraping her cast across the copper she accomplished her entry without making a noise.

Swinging her legs round she dropped to the flags and picked up her coat. It was impossible to pull the window shut from the inside, she'd have to go out and do it. Not bothering to put her coat on she ran to the back door and sped round the side of the building almost sprawling flat when she collided with the orange box.

Thank God she'd come out to close the window otherwise the box would have been left in full view of anyone who walked past. She put it back in the shed in roughly the same position she'd found it, returned to the scullery, shoved the window back where it should be and returned to the kitchen. Her teeth were chattering and she had difficulty re-bolting the door.

She'd dearly like a hot drink but daren't remain downstairs a moment longer. She wasn't sure if her shaking was from fear or cold. One thing she did know, she wasn't cut out to be a burglar or a spy, she was far too clumsy and didn't have the courage.

Her room was blessedly warm even though the fire had burned out. Stripping off her outer clothes she tumbled in to bed with her nightdress on over her vest and knickers. With the tepid hot water bottle clutched to her chest she curled in to a ball and was asleep almost immediately.

*

Jack got up early, he would do a few chores for Joan and save Hannah the unpleasant task of taking the ash bucket down to the bottom of the garden. He got the range going then cleared the fire in the bar and laid it ready for opening time. He noticed there were a few dirty glasses behind the bar, he would wash those up for Joan whilst he was about it.

His shoulder was a bit stiff but apart from that he was almost ready to return to the base. They had been unduly pessimistic about his recovery; he didn't need another week of convalescence. Donnelly wouldn't let him fly until his stitches came out and that would be at least another three of four days. He might as well make the most of it. He hardened at the thought of spending time with the girl he was already head over heels in love with.

Desperately he tried to think of something else, the weather … anything but her. He had to be realistic. She was unlikely to want to make love for a good while yet. She'd been badly damaged but he was prepared to wait, however long it took.

He dumped the tray on the washstand and looked around for a jug of water. His teeth snapped shut. He gripped the edge of the sideboard to steady himself. He couldn't believe what he saw.

He knew why the door had been unbolted, Hannah must have been outside after all and he'd locked her out. She'd had to climb in through the scullery window and that's why there were bits of plaster of paris stuck to the side of the copper.

Why the hell was she creeping about outside in the middle of the night? It didn't make any sense. He must be mistaken. She spent a lot of time in the scullery, could easily have left these bits earlier in the day. He snatched up two buckets, he'd have a look around whilst he fetched the water.

There was nothing under the scullery window that proved anything either way; if she had climbed in she would have needed a box to stand on. The idea was ludicrous. He was becoming as fanciful as an old lady. He couldn't help glancing in to the shed as he walked past but it looked exactly the same as it always did, just higgledy-piggledy piles of rubbish.

He glanced at her bike and saw her haversack was in the front pannier. He pulled it out and something heavy bumped in to his chest. He unbuckled the flap and saw the thermos flask. He unscrewed the top and tipped it over his palm, a few drops of tea splashed out. They were warm.

He sagged against the wall. For the tea to be warm it had to have been made more recently than yesterday morning. Hannah had taken a flask of tea with her. He could think of only one reason she would do that, she was meeting another bloke. Bloody hell! He'd kill the man. Then his head cleared, it couldn't be a man, she couldn't have made up the story she'd told him about being raped. Whatever it was she had been doing it was something she didn't want anyone to know about. Was she involved in the black market? She'd complained about being short of cash.

His injured shoulder meant he could only take one bucket at a time; on his first journey there was nobody else at the standpipe. On his second he met two housewives. They greeted *him* by name - he'd no idea who they were.

'Glad to see you're up and about, Flt Lt Rhodes, can't tell you how sorry we all were about your crew. Nasty business, can't think why nobody's found that murdering Nazi.'

The second woman nodded, her pink curlers bobbing beneath her headscarf. 'I reckon some traitor's hiding him, don't you Doris? He'd have given himself up otherwise, wouldn't he?'

Somehow Jack mumbled a response, filled his bucket and headed back to the pub. What those women said made sense. He couldn't bring himself to accept the obvious explanation. He wanted to punch his fist through a wall. Everything fell in to place. Hannah's mysterious absence the afternoon he'd arrived, the fact she was downstairs when he woke up last night, it must mean only one thing.

For some reason she'd decided to hide the bastard every-one was searching for. He'd much prefer it if she *was* seeing another bloke, that he *could* forgive. Angrily he brushed away his tears. He'd been so certain she was the girl for him, as honest as she was beautiful. She must have reasons she thought were valid – but it seemed to him the worst kind of betrayal.

He wouldn't confront her, she'd deny everything and then he'd never find the bastard German. He too could pretend; he'd go out with her today to fetch the cat as planned, but tonight he'd wait until she went out and then follow her. His revolver was in the bottom of his kit bag loaded and ready, he'd take it with him tonight, do it for Pete and Dave. Germans were not the only ones who could kill an enemy in cold blood.

*

Hannah appeared in the kitchen surprised to find the range already burning, the breakfast table laid and both bars ready for this evening. The back door was unlocked, Joan must be outside.

She'd dressed warmly adding a thick woolly over her cardigan and blouse. It would be cold cycling to Pond Farm to catch a cat. She was making tea when Jack came in swinging two buckets of water.

'Good grief, I didn't know you were so domesticated! You shouldn't carry anything heavy with that arm, not until your shoulder's healed.'

His eyes looked almost grey this morning, maybe being cold changed the colour. Whatever it was it made him look frightening. He must have locked her out. Had he discovered her absence?

Then he smiled and was the charming man she was coming to love. 'Morning, sweetheart, I've done everything so we can leave after breakfast. Or do you want to set the rat traps first?'

'I can't, Joan hasn't any, I'll ask Mr Boothroyd if I can borrow some of his; I'll do it when we get back. I left my haversack and flask outside the other day, I'll pop out ...'

'I brought it in; it's hanging in the scullery.' He pointed at the table. 'Sit down, I'm going to make porridge.'

Her heart sunk. 'Please, not for me. I hate the stuff, Nanny used to make me sit at the table until I'd finished. Sometimes I was there until lunchtime.'

Something odd flashed across his face, if she hadn't known better she'd have thought it disappointment.

Chapter Twelve

Joan bustled in her former animosity quite gone. 'Porridge; after bacon and eggs it's my favourite breakfast. Aren't you having any, ducks?'

'I'm sticking to toast and marmalade this morning. We're going to Pond Farm to borrow some rat traps from Mr Boothroyd, I want to set them this afternoon.'

'You're not going to church with me then?'

Hannah had been wondering why Joan was wearing a hat to breakfast but hadn't liked to ask. 'I'm sure we won't be missed, I've been in the area for several months and have never been. It would cause a stir if I turned up today.'

Joan tapped the side of her nose. 'Not ready to announce that you're courting? Don't blame you, it's nobody's business but yours.'

Jack was strangely silent, he didn't jump in to agree with their landlady's comment. She reached over and touched his arm. 'Are you sure you feel well enough to cycle three miles?'

'I'm not sleeping that's all. I expect it will be better once the funeral's over.'

Her eyes prickled. 'I wish I could come with you, I only met your crew a couple of times but I know how much they meant to you.'

'If I find the missing Nazi pilot I intend to exterminate him.'

He returned to his porridge and she continued to make toast in front of the range. He frightened her when he spoke like that; didn't he realise he'd be no better than the evil men who'd killed his friends if he shot Kurt in cold blood? Whilst he finished his meal she could make up the flask. 'Can I take a couple of slices of cake, Joan? We'll be back for lunch but it's hungry work cycling three miles.'

'Finish it up, I'm saving all the dried fruit from now on to make a Christmas cake next month. It's cold enough for Christmas already. I hope we don't get a winter like last one, we were up to our armpits in snow for months.'

'Were Betty and Ruby at the farm then?' Joan nodded. 'No wonder they thought I was worse than useless after surviving a winter like that.'

She grinned at Jack, waited for him to laugh but he seemed preoccupied this morning. Hardly surprising really when his two best friends were being buried tomorrow. She would have to tread carefully today, make sure she didn't upset him. He must be feeling some of the grief she had felt when Giles was reported missing, presumed dead.

The toasting fork shot forward and her slice of bread fell in to the flames. She felt as if she'd swallowed a large stone. Jack didn't love her, not really, he was just reacting the way she had, clutching at the nearest person who could offer him comfort. She didn't dare look at him, he would know she'd realised he was having second thoughts, regretting his impulsive declaration of love.

Quickly stuffing the bread deep in to the flames she stood up. She had lost her appetite, she made the tea and put the cake in greaseproof paper bag. Everything was in her haversack, the breakfast dishes washed and dried up, she couldn't delay their departure any longer. She was dreading the excursion, her happiness incinerated like the toast.

Jack had gone out ages ago to pump up the tyres on the decrepit bicycle. He was nowhere in sight, neither was the bicycle. Had he gone on without her? She grabbed her cycle and wheeled it out of the yard to find him waiting impatiently by the village pond.

'Sorry, I didn't mean to be so long. Have you any idea how we're going to carry a cat? I couldn't find any sacks in the shed so we'll have to use one of Mr Boothroyd's, I need to borrow traps as well.'

'I hope you don't think I'm scrambling all over the barn? I'm not risking my shoulder, I'm going to be a pallbearer tomorrow.'

It wasn't *what* he said, it was the way he phrased it that bothered her. There was no need for him to be nasty, it wasn't her fault he'd changed his mind. She stared at him thoughtfully. 'It's all right, Jack. I think we'd better get this over and done with, don't you?'

His mouth tightened and his eyes were like the North Sea. 'I'm not sure what you mean.'

'You've decided you spoke too soon. That's all right, I'm quite happy to go back to the *friendship only* arrangement we had before. I knew it was a mistake to tell you about what happened to me, no respectable man is going to want anything to do with me, I know that. Don't worry about it, I'm not going to.'

Not waiting for his reply she scrambled on her bike and shot off pedalling furiously, hoping he would think the tears streaming from her eyes were caused by the wind. All she had left was her dignity and she was determined to hang on to that.

*

Shit and derision! What should he do now? Part of him hated her for helping the German who had killed his friends but the rest still loved her and couldn't bear to see her upset. She'd been damaged enough by a man who'd mistreated her, he wasn't going to be one of them.

Today he was going to forget what he knew, time enough for recriminations tonight. He would put things right between them, he didn't want her to think he'd changed because of what that rat Mayhew had done to her. Whatever happened he would never let the authorities arrest her, somehow he'd come up with an explanation that would satisfy them. He didn't know if their relationship could survive what she'd done, but seeing her crying made him understand just what she meant to him.

Despite her attempts to get away he was soon coasting along beside her. He reached out his right hand, leaving his damaged shoulder to take the strain, and gripped her handlebars. 'Stop, Hannah, you can't rush off like that. You've got it all wrong.'

'I haven't, you've been off with me all morning, I don't blame you. Please, let's not talk about it. We can still be friends, can't we?'

This was no good, he had to speak to her before they arrived at the farm. There was only one way and he wasn't sure his injured shoulder was up to it. He dropped behind her and grabbed the back of her saddle then applied his right brake, putting both feet down to give him added leverage. 'Stop, Hannah, you don't understand.'

Instead of breaking, she pedalled harder. He couldn't hold on. He released his hold and she shot forward out of control and went sailing in to the ditch. For some reason she hadn't released her hold on the handlebars and the bike landed on top of her. The only sound was of two wheels spinning wildly in mid-air.

Bloody hell, he'd not meant to knock her off, just get her to stop. He tumbled from his bike and dived in to the ditch. He grabbed her bike, tossing it to one side where it crashed noisily on top of his own. She was lying on her back with her eyes closed, her cheeks were tearstained, her once immaculate plaster now muddied.

'Hannah, darling, are you hurt? God, I'm so sorry, I didn't mean this to happen, I just wanted you to stop so we could talk.'

Her amazing green eyes flickered open, for a second they didn't focus and then they blazed with fury. 'What on earth are you playing at, you imbecile? Haven't I had enough accidents in the past ten days without you deliberately shoving me in to the ditch like that?' She pushed him away.

'Move yourself, Flt Lt Rhodes, I would quite like to get out *if* you don't mind.'

He didn't move. Then before she could wriggle out of his grip he reached in and hauled her from the bottom of the ditch. 'Don't be ridiculous, Hannah, I've said I'm sorry. Now will you stop scowling at me and listen?'

*

How dare he call *her* ridiculous? Incensed beyond reason she lashed out at him, he lost his balance and fell flat on his back. She felt like stamping on his hand. 'I don't like you anymore, Flt Lt Rhodes, and whatever you want to say to me I don't wish to hear it. I'm going to see my friends at Pond Farm, I suggest *you* go back to the pub.'

Leaving him to pick himself up she brushed the worst of the mud from her jacket and untangled her bike from his. An ominous tinkling sound came from her haversack. 'Oh no, the flask's broken. Joan will never forgive me, she won't be able to replace it until the end of the war.'

This was too much. He put his arms round her and she fell against him. She couldn't prevent the hiccuping sobs. Forgetting she was cross with him she let him stroke her back, smooth her hair, whilst her tears soaked the shoulder of his greatcoat.

'Please, sweetheart, don't cry like this. It's only a bloody flask, for God's sake. I'll take one from the base to replace it.'

His bracing tone had the desired effect. She swallowed, sniffed and stepped back sharply forcing him to release her. Turning her back she rummaged in her jacket pocket until she found a handkerchief and noisily blew her nose. Face dry and more composed she turned. She should be thanking him for his sympathy, instead she was incensed by his lack of understanding.

'In case you'd forgotten, Jack, I broke my arm because of you and have just been sent flying from my bike for no reason at all.'

'In case *you've* forgotten, this week my best friends were shot down by a filthy German pilot and I crash landed for the second time.'

Her anger shrivelled, his contemptuous expression made her ashamed of her outburst. But she was damned if she was going to apologise again. After ramming her knitted hat on she remounted her bike. He could come, or return to The White Hart, she no longer cared what he did. She believed he hadn't rejected her because of Ralph, but he'd still changed his mind. From now on she would keep her distance, treat him like a casual acquaintance. She swallowed the lump in her throat. At least he would be away all day tomorrow at the funeral.

The farmyard was swept clean, the pigs munching contentedly on their swill and chickens and cockerels picking up spilt grain. Betty and Ruby would have finished in the milking parlour - had they been sent up to pull leeks or dig up cabbages? She hadn't spoken to Jack again and he'd made no attempt to break the silence; he remained behind her.

Leaning her cycle against the wall she headed for the farmhouse. *He* could do what he wanted but she wasn't going to invite him to come with her. Mrs Boothroyd opened the door as she approached, her happy smile made the journey worth it.

'Come in, my dear, my husband's gone over to see his sister, he'll not be back until dark.' She smiled over Hannah's shoulder. 'Don't worry about taking off your boots, Flt Lt Rhodes, we don't stand on ceremony here.'

So Jack was still behind her, she couldn't stop him following her in to the farmhouse. Her pleasure in the moment squelched beneath his boots.

'I've come to catch a cat for Joan, I'd also like to borrow some rat traps as the village shop hasn't got any at the moment.'

'Help yourself, Hannah, you know where they are. I've just taken some rock cakes out of the oven, I'm sure you'd both like one, with a nice cup of tea, before you start chasing all over the barn.'

'Thank you, Mrs Boothroyd, unfortunately I managed to break Joan's flask on the way over. I'll also need a sack to put the cat in. Is that possible?'

Hannah squirmed, her deliberate exclusion of Jack from her request seemed childish. Was it too late to mend things? She removed her jacket and it was lifted from her hand.

'I'll hang this up with mine, I expect you want to wipe some of the mud from your face before we sit down.' His voice was neutral; the teasing tone she'd become accustomed to no longer apparent.

'How kind of you to remind me, Jack. I'd quite forgotten you made me cycle in to the ditch until you mentioned it.' What their hostess thought of this stilted exchange she'd no idea, if she had a moment in privacy she would explain they'd had a row and weren't speaking. That was something Mrs B. would understand.

There was no opportunity for this as he remained firmly at her side. He was his usual charming self and after eating two rock cakes and drinking her tea she began to think she'd imagined the distance between them.

'Will Betty and Ruby be back soon?'

'They only had to take a load of hay to Wimbish, I told them to stop for a drink if it was offered. I shouldn't think they'll be much longer.'

Hannah brushed the crumbs from her lap and stood up. 'That was delicious, I didn't have any breakfast. Thank you so much. Joan says you must call in next time you come in to the village, just come round to the back door. I hope you'll take her up on the invitation.'

Mrs Boothroyd nodded vigorously. 'I certainly shall, my dear. You're a real tonic, and no mistake. I'm not going to sit around feeling sorry for myself any more, there must be hundreds of mothers who lost their sons and I bet they didn't give up like I've done these past few months.'

Jack was on his feet too. 'That was most hospitable of you, Mrs Boothroyd, I'll look forward to seeing you at The White Hart. I'm staying there at the moment, but I expect to be returning to active duty by the end of the week, if not sooner.'

Barbara felt a stab of disappointment, he couldn't make it any clearer, their brief romance was at an end. Mrs B had lost a son and he'd lost his two best friends. The world seemed a little duller, the sunshine less bright when she stepped in to the yard.

She must at least be civil to him, he couldn't help how he felt. 'Jack, I'm going to fetch the traps and a sack from the store room. Could you go and have a look in the barn and see if there's a suitable animal lurking in there?'

He straightened, bowed his head and clicked his heels. Her eyes widened, why had he chosen to do this, today of all days? 'Your wish is my command.' His mouth curved, her fear passed, he was teasing her. 'Any particular colour of cat? Sex?' His face was commendably straight as he said that but his eyes danced.

Everything was all right between them. Daringly she tilted her head to one side, placed a finger on her lips and simpered. 'Let me think? It doesn't matter about the colour and the jury is still out on the second question.'

Giggling she dodged past him and ran to the store. She could hear him chuckling to himself as he went in to the huge wooden barn. There were plenty of empty sacks piled neatly in the corner, she remembered putting them there herself. With two tucked under her arm she reached up and removed four rat traps. If these didn't work she would use poison.

As she crossed the yard she heard the clatter of hooves and rumbling cartwheels in the lane. She ran across and leant over the wall to greet her friends. 'Jack and I have come to catch a cat for Joan. Mrs B. says you can help if you want. She also said you can all have lunch in the farmhouse today, she's making soup and pasties.'

Betty expertly guided the enormous shire, Samson, through the gate. 'Blimey, wonders will never cease! Since she came back from town the other day she's been a new woman, like she was before her Sam was killed.'

'We'll not be long taking off Samson's harness, we'll join you in the barn, won't we, Betty? Be a right laugh trying to get hold of one of them barmy cats.'

Hannah removed a lump of fruit cake from her haversack, this should be enough to entice one from the beams where they lurked hissing and spitting, and occasionally peeing, on anyone unwise enough to walk beneath them.

Jack greeted her with a cheery wave. 'Up there, I've seen at least three, I suppose you want me to climb up the ladder in to the loft and try and get one for you?'

'No, we're the walking wounded; I'm going to ask Ruby to go up. She doesn't mind heights, she'll be up the ladder like a monkey on a stick.'

'Who are you calling a monkey? Cheek of it! Right, got any grub to tempt one with?'

Hannah handed over the cake. 'I thought the one that comes down first will be the friendliest. I've got a couple of sacks, if Betty waits next to you she can help you stuff it in.'

Ruby took the sacks and cake. 'I reckon the one you want is the big black tom, he often comes down after scraps. Don't you remember, he pinched your sandwich when you went to the lav the other week?'

'I do, I've heard him purring as well so he's not as unfriendly as some of them.' She stared in to the gloom of the roof; several pairs of yellow eyes stared back. It was impossible to see if the cat they wanted was up there or not. 'Here comes Betty, shall I tell her the good news?'

'Taking my name in vain? What's this news then?'

'Come on, old girl, up the ladder. We're on a mission to bag a cat. You've got to grab him with me.'

Joshing and shoving the two girls scrambled nimbly in to the hayloft. Hannah grinned at Jack. 'We'd better stand well back, you don't know what unpleasant surprises you might get if you're underneath when the cats are angry.'

Betty started crooning. 'Pussy, pussy, come and get some loverly cake. There's a good cat, come to Aunty Betty.'

Nothing happened. Ruby appeared above them. 'Here, Hannah, give us one of them pitchforks, I'll see if I can knock one off the beam, they ain't coming down to eat your cake.'

Jack handed it up. 'Be careful, I wouldn't like to be the person catching if one does fall off its perch.'

Hannah was enjoying this; they all needed, a bit of fun after so much unhappiness.

'I've come out to see what's happening. Any luck yet?'

'No, Mrs B., I think Ruby's going to try poking one with a pitchfork.'

'Oh dear! I think I'd better go and get the first aid box, I've a horrible feeling those girls are going to need it if they do that.'

Hannah held her breath, she clutched Jack's arm in her excitement and his muscles tensed. Then Ruby dislodged three cats at once and they fell on top of the girls. Betty and Ruby were screaming and swearing whilst trying to remove the scratching, spitting animals. One, a tabby, was on Ruby's head, the more she yelled the harder it gripped. Another, a black-and-white, had somehow become entangled with Betty's britches and she was dancing from foot to foot trying to shake it off.

Mrs B rocked from side to side moaning with laughter. Hannah, tears of mirth running down her cheeks, leant against Jack. She could feel his sides heaving; they could offer no advice to the beleaguered girls in the loft, they would have to sort out things for themselves. Then the third cat, the huge black tom, hurtled from the loft straight in to her arms. Instinctively she closed them as she tumbled backwards.

'Quick, Jack, get a sack. I've got the one we wanted.' She was waiting for needle sharp claws to sink in to her face but to her astonishment the cat snuggled against her, rubbing his head under her chin and purring like a sewing machine. This was a day for surprises. Slowly she sat up, stroking the animal under the chin and talking to him quietly.

The racket above them subsided, two hissing felines shot out in to the yard scattering chickens and ducks in all directions. Betty called down from above her head.

'Bloody Nora, would you look at that, Ruby? Hannah's sitting there as pleased as punch, not so much as a scratch anywhere, the blooming cat in her lap as happy as larry.'

'I think he likes me, he knows I've come to take him somewhere nice and warm where he'll get plenty to eat and not have to share.'

Jack dropped down to his haunches beside her shaking his head in disbelief. 'How about that? He came to you. Quite unbelievable. Clever boy ...' he reached out to stroke the cat and instantly it changed. A deep rumbling growl echoed round the barn, Hannah could feel it tensing, ready to pounce.

'Don't touch him, he obviously doesn't like men. I'll wait until Betty's down and then she can hold him whilst I find him a nice warm box.'

He answered from a good yard away. 'Not putting him in a sack?'

'There, pussy, the nasty man has gone away. He wants me to put you in a smelly old bag, I wouldn't do that to you, now would I?'

Betty and Ruby slid down the ladder still muttering. 'You owe us a double on Saturday, Hannah. Fancy laughing at us when we was being attacked.'

'I think Joan will buy you a double each when she meets this fine young man. Here, will one of you take him whilst I get up?'

They backed away shaking their heads. 'Not likely, I'm not going anywhere near any cat ever again. Put us off for life, ain't it Ruby?'

'Here, my dear, I'll take him. Betty there's a cardboard box in the outhouse, why don't you get that for us?' Mrs Boothroyd reached down and the cat was transferred like a large, black, furry parcel.

Hannah sprang to her feet and picked up one of the dropped sacks. 'This can go in the bottom of the box, it'll give him something to hang on to when we're bumping back along the lane.'

Jack scowled at the animal. 'Do you think a box will stay on the back of your bike? It would be much easier if he was in a sack.'

Laughing at his disgust, she held out her arms and the cat sprang across, purring loudly. 'I'm going to call him Sooty, what do you think?'

'I'm going to call him Dangerous, and I hope he stays

outside. Can't imagine anything worse than being attacked by *that* in the middle of the night.'

She pulled the contented animal's ears. 'He's going to be an indoor cat, Joan's overrun with mice in the house, that's where he's needed. And anyway he's likely to run off if he's let out too soon.'

The box was tied securely to the rear of her bicycle and the sack put in the bottom. However, Sooty refused to leave her arms; when she tried to put him in he burrowed further in to her jacket clinging on with his claws. 'I'm going to have to carry him, I think if I open my jacket he can go inside and be perfectly safe.'

This proved to be the case, in spite of the bumping and jolting the animal hung on and didn't stop purring once. She left Jack to put her bike away and carried Sooty in to the larder. There was no sign of Joan, perhaps she'd gone to lunch with one of her friends after church. The cat still refused to budge, she began to think she would be carrying him around like a baby for the rest of the day.

'I've filled up an old wooden tray I found in the shed - it will do as dirt box until you can let him out. Do want me to put it in here?'

'Please, I'm trying to get him to come out of my jacket but he won't move. Could you get him a saucer of milk and a bit of bacon rind? With any luck he's hungry and will get down to eat.'

Eventually Sooty left his refuge, the enticement of a piece of bacon all to himself did the trick. As soon as he was down Hannah shot out of the larder and closed the door behind her. 'I'm going to leave Joan a note, make sure she doesn't let him out inadvertently. I'm going to have some of the soup she made yesterday, would you like some?'

'Not now, I'm still full of rock cake. I'm going to have a lie down, after all the excitement I'm knackered. If you leave it out, I'll heat it up later on when I get up.'

The kitchen door closed leaving her alone in the kitchen. She didn't understand him at all, one minute he was nasty, the next nice. She couldn't sort things out at the moment. Time enough to mend fences with Jack when Kurt was safe

Chapter Thirteen

There seemed little point in writing a note about the cat in the larder, Hannah intended to spend the afternoon in the kitchen anyway. Mrs B. had put a miscellany of vegetables and six fresh eggs in the box that was intended for Sooty. She would make a vegetable stew for supper and jam roly-poly for dessert as soon as she'd finished her lunch.

She was sitting at the kitchen table reading an old copy of The News Chronicle, the pudding gently steaming in a cloth in a saucepan and the stew bubbling beside it, listening to the clock ticking. Joan was having a long lunch, it must be after three thirty. Jack was obviously avoiding her, he couldn't still be asleep.

The newspaper was spread out on the table in front of her; something tiny, shiny and black dropped on to it. She saw it hop. My God! A flea! She looked at her jumper, the surface was moving. With a shriek of horror she kicked her chair back so violently it crashed to the flagstones. Ignoring it she raced the back door, flung it open and once outside stripped off her jumper.

There were little black dots in her cardigan as well. Frantically she unbuttoned it and tossed it aside, her blouse and vest followed leaving only a brassiere between her and the biting wind. Would her slacks be infested too? She hesitated, she couldn't bear the thought of having anything next to her skin that was alive with fleas. She unbuttoned the waistband and stepped out of her trousers.

Her skin was goose bumped, her teeth beginning to chatter. She stared hopelessly at the pile of clothes; she didn't want to touch them but she could hardly leave them outside. Then the back door flew open and Jack appeared.

*

Hannah's scream and the crash of a chair falling jerked Jack from his novel. He was on his feet and halfway down the corridor before it stopped. His socks skidded on the boards. There was no time to go back and put his boots on, she'd sounded desperate. He burst in to the kitchen, a blast of icy air greeted him. The back door was wide open. What the hell was going on?

He slid to the door - his eyes widened and a wave of heat engulfed him. She was standing shivering in her knickers and bra. He'd never seen anything so desirable in his life. 'For God's sake, Hannah, what the hell are you doing?'

'Fleas, the cat's infested. So was I. Joan will kill me, first I broke her flask and now I've brought fleas in to the house.'

Forgetting he had no shoes on he closed the gap between them, slid his good arm under her knees, and scooped her up. 'Inside, don't wriggle or I'll drop you.' Her teeth were clattering like a pair of castanets, her skin turning blue, she'd be lucky she didn't catch pneumonia after this.

Not stopping in the kitchen he shouldered his way in to the passage and somehow negotiated the staircase without mishap. Thank God her door was ajar, he strode in and dumped her unceremoniously on her bed. Snatching up the eiderdown he dragged it around her shoulders.

'Sit there, you blithering idiot, whilst I light the fire.' It was difficult to strike a match with his hand shaking so much. Knowing she was sitting all but naked on the bed was playing havoc with his pulse. Whatever she was, whatever she'd done, he wanted to make love to her. He daren't turn round, his erection was painfully obvious.

He had to get out of there before he did something he would be ashamed of for the rest of his life. Keeping his back to her, he stood up. 'Get dressed, then come down and have a hot drink. We've got to do something about that damned cat before Joan gets back.'

*

The door closed shut. He was being beastly again. Treating her like a naughty schoolgirl and it served her right. What had she been thinking of? It had been sheer madness to strip outside. She shuddered. She had an absolute horror of crawly things on her skin, this was irrational but she couldn't help it. Betty wasn't too keen on spiders, Ruby hated snakes and lizards, with her it was lice and fleas - in fact anything that invaded her space. Cockroaches, bedbugs, she hated them all.

She wasn't too keen on him either. What a nerve, to call her a *blithering idiot*. She must get dressed. He might be an overbearing, arrogant man but she was forced to admit on this occasion he was absolutely right. They *had* to do something about Sooty before the whole place was overrun. The larder was so cold there was a good chance the fleas would remain on their host.

By the time she was dressed her teeth had stopped chattering and she was more than ready for a cup of tea. She dithered in her bedroom, the thought of facing him after she'd displayed herself so brazenly made her nervous. She couldn't go down, he'd have to … no, Sooty hated him, she had no option but to face her embarrassment. With the metal nit comb clutched in one hand and a piece of wet soap in the other she reluctantly left the safety of her room. She was almost at the head of the stairs when he roared up them.

'Hannah, if you don't come down this minute, I'm coming to get you.'

'There's no need to shout, I'm here now. I hope the tea's not stewed.' She sounded churlish but didn't care. Keeping her head lowered she stomped in to the kitchen and picked up the nearest mug of tea. The sound of the range burning and her slurping filled the kitchen. She couldn't put it off. Raising her head, her cheeks burning, she glared at him. To her astonishment he was lounging back on a chair, his long legs folded at the ankle, his arms crossed on his chest and his mouth twitching with amusement.

'Don't you dare laugh, it's not at all funny. I have a thing about fleas, I couldn't help myself.'

'No need to apologise on my account, it's not often a chap gets to look at a beautiful young woman in her underwear.'

Her mug thumped down on the table and she sprang at him. He was too quick for her, somehow managed to be on his feet and able to fend her off. 'I hate you, you're despicable. A gentleman wouldn't she have mentioned what happened.'

Laughing down at her, he gently pushed her back in to her seat. 'I never professed to be a gentleman, I'm just an ordinary bloke. I'm sorry if I upset you. Calm down and finish your tea, we've got to do something about that dratted animal in a minute.'

Bristling with indignation she finished her tea in one swallow. 'Right, we need to spread the newspaper on the table. When the fleas hop off you've got to catch them in the soap. When I've combed him, I'll cover him with Deris Powder, that should do the trick. I suppose there's no point in asking you to go and get Sooty?'

'None at all. In case you're wondering where your clothes are, I've put them in the copper and tipped a bucket of water over them. With any luck the little buggers will drown.'

'Thank you.' She moved towards the larder door but couldn't bring herself to open it. The thought of picking up the cat, of having more fleas on her clothes rooted her to the spot. Somehow she forced her hand to the latch.

'No, sorry, I'm a brute. I didn't realise, it's not disgust it's terror, isn't it?' She nodded, too sick to speak.

'What we need is something to put over our clothes, I bet Joan has some aprons somewhere.'

Anything rather than having to hold the cat. Her skin was still crawling from the fleas she'd picked up before even though she'd checked thoroughly and there were none on her. 'I'm sure she has a couple of spares we can use.'

Seeing him wrapped in a floral pinny, his broad shoulders jutting out, the material barely stretching over his chest, made her smile.

'That's better. I've had a brainwave, if you stand at the far end of the table, I can open the door and hide behind it. With any luck the wretched animal will jump on the table in order to reach you.'

The cat was plaintively mewing and scratching the door, the upset had obviously distressed him. 'Right, everything's ready here. I've sprinkled Deris Powder on the newspaper, hopefully that and the soap will be enough to keep the horrible things on the table.'

Jack lifted the latch and pulled the door against him. Sooty shot out but instead of jumping on the table he hurtled under it launching himself on to Hannah's legs. His ears were flat on his head, she could feel his body trembling as he scrabbled his way up, his pitiful crying overcame her fear of infestation.

'Come here, poor old thing. See, there's nothing to worry about. I'm going to give you a lovely comb and get rid of all your little visitors.' The cat purred and nudged her under the chin. She carefully placed him in the centre of the newspapers, stroking him and talking to him the whole time.

With her plaster cast resting on his back she began to drag the metal prongs through his fur starting with his head. 'Look, he seems to like it. Do you think he knows we're trying to help him?'

'Probably, I actually like cats, prefer them to dogs. I don't know why this one has taken against me.'

As Hannah dislodged the fleas in their hundreds he was hard put to catch them on his soap. 'Dip it in the saucer of water, it'll keep it sticky.' He did as she suggested. Sooty was purring again, his ears pricked and apart from giving Jack a stony stare occasionally, the cat ignored him.

Half an hour later the job was done. She picked Sooty up and went to sit in the wooden rocking chair by the range.

'There, pussycat, nice and clean. Aunty Joan wouldn't want you in here with fleas.' The animal kneaded her stomach with sheathed claws. 'It's so cold in the larder, I don't want to put him back in there.'

He grinned. 'You're too soft-hearted. He's been living outside all his life, the larder will seem like a palace after that.'

'I think I'll find him an old bit of blanket then he'll have something to snuggle in to tonight.' She pointed to the two saucepans. 'Could you take them off the heat, please? Leave the stew with the lid on but the roly-poly needs to be lifted out and put on a plate.' His mock salute made her laugh.

'This whatever it is in the muslin smells delicious; is it for tonight?'

'It is. You must be famished, you didn't have any lunch.'

Light footsteps outside announced the arrival of their landlady. The cat tensed and swivelled his head to watch the door. Hannah shared his nervousness. Too late to wonder if Joan actually liked cats, something she should have asked before she'd brought one home.

The door opened and Joan stepped in shaking the rain from her umbrella. 'It's turned nasty, freezing cold rain …'

Sooty launched himself from Hannah's lap and with one spring arrived at Joan's feet. 'My word, what have we here?' Dropping her umbrella in a heap she bent down and scooped the cat up. 'What a lovely animal. Is he for me?'

'He is, we thought he could catch the mice for you. I've called him Sooty.'

'That's why you both went to Pond Farm. Thank you, I never thought to get a cat; my old man doesn't take to them much. But he's away, possibly for years, so I can please myself.' She tickled the happy animal under his chin. 'Here, ducks, you hold him for me whilst I get my coat off.' She sniffed his fur and nodded. 'Given him a good going over with the Deris Powder, I expect he was riddled with fleas.'

'He was. Hannah has a horror of them and she was smothered in the little blighters, she stripped off her clothes and I've put them in the copper to soak.'

'Put a cup of vinegar in the water and give it a stir, ducks, that'll shift them. It's washday tomorrow, you can give me a hand and we'll get them nice and clean for you.'

Hannah put the cat down on the flagstones and immediately it stalked across the floor, tail as stiff as a bottle brush as if he owned the place already. He jumped nimbly in to the rocking chair, curled up and promptly went to sleep.

Joan smiled happily at her new pet. 'Bless him, he's making himself at home. It doesn't seem possible he's been living wild, he's as friendly as anything.' She sniffed appreciatively. 'My, someone's been busy. I've got a lovely bit of liver here but I'll put it in the meat safe for tomorrow seeing as you've got tea already cooked for us.'

'All I've got to do is make some custard, you've got some Bird's on the shelf I can use and we've got plenty of milk left.'

*

The pub was quiet, just a few locals drifted in for a quick half and a game of darts. It was too wet for any of the personnel from the base to cycle over.

'Run along, ducks, no point in you being down here tonight. Your young man was very quiet at tea this evening - don't blame him. I'm not surprised he's gone up early. It's going to be awful for him tomorrow.'

'It was hearing the planes go out, it's the first sortie since Pete and Dave were killed. I know he thinks he should be back on duty avenging them by killing as many Germans as possible. He said he's going to look for the pilot himself.'

Joan tutted. 'That's bad, he'll come to grief if he carries on bearing a grudge. This is the first time in my life I'm glad I wasn't blessed with children.' She sighed. 'I reckon there's other folk going to go out looking. Feeling's still running high around the village.'

Hannah hid her concern and paused at the door. 'He told me he's a pall bearer, he shouldn't be doing that, he's still got stitches in his shoulder.'

'Can't stop him, best to let him get on with it. If he makes himself unwell then he's got you to take care of him when he gets back. A car's coming for him first thing, he'll be gone before you come down for breakfast.'

'Goodnight, Joan. Shall I make you a bottle and put it in your bed when I go up?'

'Not to worry, I'm going to have a cup of tea and talk to my new friend when I finish here. I reckon I'll be able to close by ten o'clock. We're all going to get an early night for once.'

Upstairs was quiet, Jack must be asleep already. Joan was right – Kurt wasn't safe in the cottage anymore.

She must get him away tonight – tomorrow might be too late.

After her close shave the other night she wondered whether to get in to her nightdress and put her outdoor clothes back on top. That way if she was seen it would just look like she'd been outside to use the lavatory. But she decided against it, she didn't want to give the German any ideas. Poor man, he'd have no hot drink tonight. Joan had been remarkably phlegmatic about the loss of her precious flask, she'd said Sooty was more than worth it. The fact Jack had promised to replace it had also helped soften the blow.

Tonight she would take what was left of the vegetable stew in a Kilner jar, she'd deliberately left the saucepan on top of the range to keep warm. Jack had devoured three helpings of jam roly-poly and custard, so there was none of that to take. There were still the uneaten slices of fruit cake left over from this morning, that would be treat enough.

She waited an hour after she'd heard Joan go to bed before venturing out. She forgotten about the cat, Joan hadn't shut him in the larder but left the door open in the hope that he would hear the mice and go in and catch them. The animal greeted her with rapturous purring, weaving in and out of her feet in delight.

'Shush, pussy, I've got to go out. You be a good boy and catch lots of mice for Aunty Joan.'

With the warm stew safely tucked inside her haversack, the plum cake, two slices of bread and cheese, plus a hard-boiled egg there was more than enough food to last Kurt for two or three days.

It had stopped raining, thank God; it would be hard to explain a sodden jacket hanging on the peg in the scullery tomorrow morning. Carefully extricating the heavy bicycle Jack had used that morning she wheeled it in to the road glad the ground was wet, it made things much quieter underfoot.

The bike was hard work to push and twice she walked through large puddles and regretted not putting on her gumboots. Her haversack was much heavier than usual, the glass jar full of stew weighed a ton. Leaning the cycle in the shadow of the rear wall of the cottage she pushed open the door and called softly in to the darkness.

'Kurt, Flt Lt Schumann, I'm sorry, but you have to leave tonight.' She almost wet herself when he replied from beside her.

'I am ready, Fraulein, I shall be glad to leave this Debfield where everybody seems determined to kill me on sight.'

His criticism hurt. 'You would feel exactly the same if two if your best friends had been shot down in cold blood. They don't know it wasn't you that did it - to them you're the worst kind of Nazi murderer.'

He was obviously offended. She could see from the dim light of her torch that he stiffened, she felt a flicker of fear remembering the gun he'd waved at her the first time they had met a few days ago. Then he clicked his heels quite audibly and bowed. It reminded her sharply of Jack's parody of a German officer.

'My apologies, I have no right to comment on this matter. You have risked your life to keep me safe. And you are probably correct, I should no doubt feel exactly the same if I was in the position of your RAF personnel.' Thank goodness, she wasn't sure she could deal with him when he was icily correct. Then he nodded again and continued. 'However, I must point out that what my compatriots did to your friends has been done several times to officers of my acquaintance by your RAF gunners. We are not the only ones who use unpleasant tactics. It's kill or be killed.'

This conversation had gone on long enough. She didn't want to know that the pleasant young men she'd met in the bar were just as capable of shooting down an unprotected man at the end of a parachute as the German Luftwaffe. War was a ghastly thing, it changed nice men on both sides in to monsters.

'I'm sure you're right but there's no time to debate it now. You must leave, I have a bicycle outside and you can take my haversack as well. I expect you heard the planes go out earlier, they'll be back any time. If you can get to another area you can pretend to have been shot down tonight. They'll never know the difference.'

She dumped the bag on the floor between them; she would worry about explaining its loss once he was away safely. He was dressed in his uniform, his leather flying jacket ideal camouflage in the darkness.

'I have buried the sacks in the garden, I am certain no one will know I have ever been in this cottage if they do come and look here again. I have also removed the stitches from my head. Do you know in which direction I should cycle?'

'Head south; turn left when you get to the main street, follow the lane for about two miles and then turn left again at the junction. With luck you should be several miles away before anybody finds you. Could I ask you to stop somewhere and eat your stew? Then you must leave the jar, it's the only thing that might identify me.' She gestured to the haversack. 'This time I've just dropped the food in, not wrapped it, it will look as if you've stolen it from someone's kitchen. I'm sure you must have similar haversacks in Germany.'

'Indeed we have. I shall do as you suggest. I promise no one will know of your involvement from me. I only have to give my name, rank, and number. I'm not required to tell the authorities anything else.'

Now the time for him to leave had arrived she was strangely reluctant to see him go. There was something about this tall, spare, young man that appealed to her. If they had met under different circumstances, before she'd met Jack, they might have been more than friends.

He picked up the haversack in one hand. She was unsure if she should embrace him, wish him good luck. She took a hesitant step forward. Good God, he had his revolver in his other hand and was pointing it at the door. With a stifled scream she spun to see a dark shape silhouetted in the entrance. Before she could intervene this man raised a gun and fired.

She screamed as Kurt fell backwards. She dropped to her knees beside him. His jacket was covered in blood. His eyes were closed. He was dead.

Chapter Fourteen

Someone was screaming. The room stank of cordite. She was alone with a murderer.

'For God's sake, Hannah, don't make that racket. Go home; get away from here before anyone arrives.'

She was wrenched to her feet. Her head snapped forward and she bit her tongue. The sharp pain focused her mind. Had she been making the noise? What was Jack doing here? He shook her again.

'Kurt is dead. He's been murdered. Why would anyone do that?'

The grip on her shoulders tightened cruelly. 'It was him or me. You've been harbouring an enemy. Get out of here or I might change my mind and hand you to the authorities.'

Reality made her knees buckle. She lashed out, her heavy work shoe connected with his shin and he reeled back letting her go. '*You* are worse than the Germans. *They* were killed in battle, *you* sneaked in like a coward and shot Kurt. I know who my enemy is.'

Her stomach roiled and she staggered to a corner and was violently sick. There was nothing more she could do for poor Kurt. She wiped her mouth on her sleeve, straightened and stepped away from the mess. She heard loud voices and running footsteps. She couldn't face the questioning, she must get away. 'You're contemptible. You're not worthy of my love.' She stopped to steady her voice. 'Even Ralph Mayhew would be preferable as a partner.'

He raised his arm but she ducked under it and fled. She ran in to the fields not stopping until her chest was too tight to breathe. Collapsing to her knees she buried her face in her hands and rocked in her grief. She was crying for Kurt but also for the death of her dreams.

The cold seeping in to her slacks roused her from her stupor. She was so cold; she wasn't sure where she was. Was she facing the village or away from it? Her fingers, even with thick gloves on, were stiff with cold.

Silence surrounded her, not even the hoot of an owl to keep her company. Where was her torch? She'd never get to the pub without it. She was so tired—perhaps if she lay down again for a while she'd feel better. Slowly she sank back to the wet soil and let the darkness take her.

*

He couldn't go after Hannah; villagers were almost at the cottage. Jack shone his torch around the room. Bloody hell - the haversack! He snatched it up and slung it over his shoulder as PC Smith poked his head through the door.

'What's going on in here?' His hat and jacket were on but his pyjama collar was visible beneath his uniform.

Jack stepped aside to show the body of the missing pilot. 'I found him here, I had to shoot him. The blighter deserved it.'

'No quarrel with that, Flt Lt Rhodes, but we heard a girl screaming just after.'

Jack swallowed; he'd forgotten she'd been screaming blue murder. What the hell could he say to explain Hannah's presence at the cottage?

The bobby stepped in followed by several other men all

more or less dressed. 'Out for a bit of courting? Don't worry, we'll not think the worse of you. Must have been a bit of a shock for the young lady coming face-to-face with a Nazi.'

He'd been given the answer. 'Exactly, you know Mrs Stock- she's put us at opposite ends of the building.'

A murmur of sympathy rippled round the group. Then someone a little brighter than the rest spoke out.

'You always carry a loaded revolver with you when you go out courting?'

'When there's a murdering Nazi on the loose I do.' Jack pointed to the gun still gripped in the German's hand. 'I was hoping we might come across him. It's the only reason I suggested we go out for a bike ride in the middle of the night.' He hoped his half smile and nonchalant tone was convincing. 'Hannah didn't want to come but I persuaded her it was romantic.' He patted the haversack hanging from his shoulder. 'Even got a midnight feast packed up.'

The clever dick shoved his way through the group and stood, chin thrust forward, fists clenched menacingly. 'No blanket? Don't reckon any young lady round here would agree to a bit of how's your father without something to sit on.'

Jack closed the gap between them. He was a stone heavier and a head taller and used all of it to his advantage. The man's bravado wilted. 'I hope you're not suggesting we intended to do anything improper?' His hand snaked out and gripped the man's throat. 'I'll not have you bad-mouthing my fiancée.'

The constable intervened hastily. 'That's quite enough of that. Here, Tom, you get off out of here. I don't want any more trouble tonight.'

The cowed man slunk off; Jack was light headed with relief. No one suspected Hannah had anything to do with this, as far as they were concerned she was an innocent bystander. Could he wriggle out of it as easily? How many people would also think he was a cold-blooded murderer?

'Right, young man, leave everything to me. You're a bleedin' hero, the beggar might have shot your young lady if you hadn't been ready.' A chorus of approval rippled round the group. One stepped forward to slap Jack on the back. 'The doc's on his way. Get yourself home and check your young lady's not upset, not every day your boyfriend shoots a German.'

'I'll do that, thank you, constable. You know where I am. I can't give a statement tomorrow; it's the funeral in Cambridge. Please don't interview Hannah either; she'll need a day to get over this.'

'Fair enough.' He offered his hand. 'Every man here thinks you've done a right good job.'

They shook hands. He left but collapsed against the cottage wall until he stopped shaking. Where the hell was his revolver? He didn't remember much after pulling the trigger. He must've dropped it. He'd never use it like that again—seeing the shock on the German's face as the bullet entered his chest would stay in his head forever.

When he'd arrived Hannah was looking up at the man wearing the hated Luftwaffe uniform. His head had boiled with images of Pete and Dave dangling helplessly whilst this man machine-gunned them, but he hadn't intended to kill him. The man had pointed a gun; his own finger had closed on the trigger instinctively. If it hadn't, he'd be dead. Knowing this didn't make him feel any better.

He should be pleased his friends were avenged but he was sick and ashamed. Hannah's words rang in his ears. She was right—what he'd done *was* despicable. He should have called out. Maybe the man wasn't intending to fire. He should have given him a chance.

Joan was in the kitchen when he got back. 'What's going on? All that racket in the street woke me. I checked your room so I knew you were out. You look dreadful, white as a sheet, sit down and I'll make you a cuppa.'

There was something he had to do, something urgent, but he couldn't think what this was.

When he felt better he was sure he'd remember. He couldn't speak until he'd finished his tea; Joan waited patiently, rocking back and forth with the huge black tomcat purring on her lap.

He'd spilt a lot of his tea but his hands were steady now. He could think of no easy way to tell Joan. 'I just shot the missing German. He was waiting with a gun. I've been going out every night to look for him.'

She frowned and pointed to the haversack that hung from the chair back next to him. 'Why did you take food with you? I don't understand.'

He shoved himself to his feet. 'Joan, did Hannah come in a while back?'

'No, I've been here for an hour. Jack—you've not left her out there on her own?'

'She ran off then the local bobby arrived and I stayed to explain. I thought she was in bed.'

How could he have forgotten Hannah? No wonder Joan was glaring at him.

'I'll get dressed and fetch a blanket. Make a bottle, there's a spare one in the scullery. I'm coming with you, I know this area like the back of my hand and we'll find her quicker together.' She returned a thick scarf tied firmly around her head and a blanket over her arm.

'We were at the deserted cottage,' Jack said.

'Well, if you didn't pass her on the way home there's only one way she can have gone and that's out in to the fields. I hope she's all right. Otherwise you'll have a second death on your conscience.'

*

Someone was shaking her, calling her name. Hannah ignored

them, she didn't want to wake up, far better to stay asleep. Then something warm was shoved inside her jacket and she was on her feet. Next she was cocooned in a blanket and picked up. He smelt familiar – safe. She relaxed and went back to sleep.

He wouldn't let her rest and someone else was with him. They were stripping off her clothes; she should protest about this but was too lethargic to bother.

First one leg and then the other was being rubbed so hard it hurt. Her eyes opened. She wasn't in the field but lying on her bed and Joan was the one doing the rubbing.

'Good girl, wake up now for your Aunty Joan. Jack's gone to fetch a hot drink and some more bottles. You got ever so cold out there, you need to get moving again. Cold can kill you stone dead if you're not careful.'

The word *dead* sent shockwaves through Hannah's body. She jack-knifed and clutched Joan's hands. 'Jack shot the German. He's dead. How could he do that? How could he shoot someone like that? Don't let him anywhere near me; he's a monster, worse than any Nazi.'

'There, there, ducks. Don't get upset. I'll tell him to leave tomorrow; I don't want him under my roof anymore not after what he did.'

'You agree with me?'

Joan's mouth twisted. 'I don't care about the German; it's what Jack *didn't* do that's upset me. He came waltzing in here and drank a mug of tea and then asked whether you were safe in bed. It doesn't bear thinking of, if we hadn't found you, you would have died. I'm disappointed in him.'

A hesitant knock on the door interrupted them. Hannah shrank back pulling the blankets round her. Joan stalked to the door and flung it open. 'Give us the bottles and the tea, Flt Lt Rhodes, then get yourself to bed. Pack your things. I don't want you back here after the funeral.'

'I understand, Mrs Stock. I've given this address to PC

Smith and the authorities want to interview me on Tuesday. They'll come here. I'm sorry, but I have to be here that morning. That will be the last time. I hope that's acceptable.'

He sounded broken, the misery in his voice brought tears to Hannah's eyes. Everything had gone wrong; she wished the last ten days had never happened. Two good men had died in a horrible way and then a third had been murdered by the man she loved but never wanted to speak to again. The pain was worse than anything she'd experienced, worse than the aftermath of Mayhew's dreadful attack.

*

'Very well, return for your interview. If you're gallivanting around the place shooting people and letting Hannah almost freeze to death then you should be on active duty if you want my opinion.'

He didn't. 'I'll move to my billet on the base. Don't worry, Mrs Stock, I'll be flying in the next operation.'

He trudged to his room, it no longer seemed cosy and welcoming but a prison, the walls pressing in on him. Joan was right, the sooner he got back in the air the better for everyone. He flopped on his bed without removing his boots or outer clothes.

His life was in tatters, his best friends dead and his newfound love crushed by circumstances beyond both their control. He yawned; another few hours and he had to be up and waiting for the car coming to collect him.

The evening's events drifted through his mind. He'd told the constable Hannah was his fiancée, he'd have to put that straight tomorrow night. One thing he *was* pleased about, he'd kept her involvement quiet. Hopefully Joan would forget about the haversack.

His eyes were damp as he rolled over and pulled the eiderdown across his legs. He'd met the girl of his dreams last week, had cartwheeled from love to hate and back again. One thing he was sure of, she hated *him* and he could never forgive *her*. But this didn't stop him loving her, desiring her. God - how he hated this bloody war.

*

Hannah finished her second cup of tea and realised she wanted to spend a penny. She wasn't going outside again tonight. Joan had gone down to make more tea and left the tray on the bedside table along with some ginger nuts.

She'd had to march around the room until her hands and feet were warm. She couldn't believe Jack had shot Kurt. No, *hands up*, just straight in and bang - the German was dead

She slid under the blankets; her toes were on one hot water bottle another was on her tummy and a third at her back—blissfully warm. How had Jack had appeared so suddenly? Had he known last night? Was that why he'd changed towards her yesterday?

How had he pretended all day everything was all right when he was planning to murder an innocent man? She didn't know him at all; he wasn't the man she'd thought he was. Then she remembered his smiling eyes, the way his mouth quirked when he was teasing her, how he'd carried her back from the field cradling her against his damaged shoulder.

Why hadn't the police come? She expected to be arrested. Had he told them she'd been hiding Kurt? A wave of nausea engulfed her. Her haversack—when they found it beside the body they would know one of them had been harbouring an enemy. It wasn't Jack,so even someone as dim as PC Smith would work it out.

This was her last night of freedom. Tomorrow she'd be taken to prison No-one would care when she told them Kurt hadn't shot Pete and Dave, that Kurt was an educated man no different from them. Germans were painted with the same brush; they were evil Nazis, they deserved to die and so did anyone who helped them.

She couldn't sleep. Downstairs she raked the range, riddled it, and threw on a hod full of coal. This was shameful extravagance but she wasn't going to spend her last night shivering. She lit two oil lamps and carried one in to the larder to collect milk and the tin of cocoa. Her foot squelched on something soft and she almost dropped the lamp.

She expected to see cat mess stuck to her slipper. Instead there was a neat row of dead mice. Sooty purred around her legs waiting for praise. 'Well done, clever cat. I can't believe you've caught so many. Aunty Joan will be thrilled. I'll let you in to the shed in the morning to catch the rats.'

It would be dawn soon; she didn't intend to be here when Jack arrived. He'd be down half an hour before the car came. An envelope addressed to him was placed prominently in the centre of the table leaning against the sugar bowl. Joan had given him a refund.

She'd wash her mug, damp down the range and go back to bed. The orange glow from the oil lamp filled the freezing scullery. As she was drying it her eyes drifted to the pegs by the door.

Her fingers slackened and the mug smashed on the flagstones. The cat shot off hissing and spitting. Hanging next to her jacket was her missing haversack. Jack had brought it back. Could this mean she wouldn't be arrested in the morning?

Chapter Fifteen

Jack shaved in cold water and nicked his cheek several times. Better that than meeting either Joan or Hannah whilst he waited for the kettle to boil. He glanced around the room, his kit bag was packed, he only had to strip the bed and he was ready to leave.

His boots needed polishing and his greatcoat was covered in mud but he could sort himself out in his rooms at the base. When more than one bloke was buried most of the squadron, including the ground crew, attended.

He would nip in to see Hugh first and get the stitches removed. Then he would persuade Wing Commander Stanton he was fit for duty. That's if they'd found a replacement kite and crew for him.

The kitchen was warm, the range hardly needed filling. He had thirty minutes before the car arrived so he'd make himself tea and toast. Sadly he pocketed the envelope. This was a refund. Nothing could be plainer; he wouldn't even be welcome for a drink at The White Hart.

The cat ignored him but there was the occasional rumbling purr when he walked past. Amazing how the animal had adapted to domesticity, one would have thought he'd been living in the lap of luxury all his life. He took all four water buckets to the stand pipe and filled them. That was one job less for Hannah. Once his crockery was washed there was nothing left to do. He might as well wait outside.

Looking around for the last time his mouth tightened, this wasn't how it should have been. He removed the photograph and lock of hair from his pocket—he'd no right to these anymore. A shiver of apprehension flickered down his spine. Was he jinxing himself by giving up his lucky charm?

He hefted his kit bag over his shoulder and marched out. He was suicidal already, God knows how he'd be after the funeral.

*

Hannah was dressed when he left. She pulled back the black-out and watched him toss his kit bag in to the miniscule back seat of the MG sports car that had come to collect him. She'd cried enough over him. He was gone - she had to get on with her life.

Confident she could go downstairs without further upset she crept through the empty pub. It wasn't really empty, Joan was still here, but without Jack it wouldn't be the same.

Her eyes were gritty from lack of sleep. The pub wasn't opening today out of respect so there was nothing to do in the bars. Betty and Ruby didn't know about last night, she must cycle over and tell them. She didn't want to be here today with time to brood. She'd go if Joan didn't want her help with the laundry.

Sooty greeted her by leaping from the rocking chair in to her arms, the candle went flying and the room was plunged in to darkness. 'Blasted cat! Look what you've done, it's a good thing I wasn't carrying a full pot.'

He crawled up her jumper and hung over her shoulder, his purring practically deafened her. As her eyes became accustomed to the dark she realised the range was made up. Little point trying to remove the cat, he just unsheathed his claws and hung on. He smelt fragrant enough but she didn't like him so close to her face in case he still had fleas.

She removed the mantle from the oil lamp on the table and lit the wick. The envelope of money had gone but in its place was the folded paper with her lock of hair and the small, grainy photograph she'd given Jack. Her stomach lurched. He shouldn't have given these back—they were his good luck charms.

She glanced at the clock - quarter past seven - the funeral wasn't until eleven o'clock. If she left now she could reach the base before the cortege left and leave them at the guardhouse. 'Get down, Sooty, I've got to run upstairs and write a letter.'

This time he allowed her to remove him and seemed content to remain in the kitchen. She was on her way back with her leather writing folder under her arm when she realised there was no rush, Jack wouldn't need the lock of hair or photograph until he returned. It would be better not to risk seeing him face-to-face.

There was plenty of time to fill the copper and light the fire under it so everything was ready for when Joan came down. Her foot knocked against a bucket and an icy stream of water shot down her leg. She hadn't expected them to be full; he must have gone out in the dark and done that before he left. If he hadn't killed Kurt last night there might be a chance they could sort things out. He probably felt the same way about a traitor as she did about a killer. It didn't seem possible she could still love him after what he'd done, but she did.

By the time the copper was full the kettle was whistling. She drank her tea whilst writing a note telling Jack to keep the hair and photograph, to think of them as his personal rabbit's foot. She thanked him for bringing back the haversack and wished him well in the future. This was hard to compose, her words were smudged and blotched when she'd finished.

'Good morning, ducks, at least it's not raining, that's

something. Aren't you having any breakfast? I could do you a nice egg and fried bread.'

'I couldn't eat anything, thanks. I've filled up the copper and lit the fire; Jack fetched the water for you before he left. That was kind of him, wasn't it?'

Joan sniffed. 'Least he could do, but I'll not say anything as it'll upset you.' The rattle of the letterbox at the end of the passageway interrupted their conversation. 'I'll get the letters, you dry your eyes and make yourself a bit of toast, there's a good girl.'

She returned with an important looking white envelope addressed to Hannah. 'There's one for you, it's got a Saffron Walden postmark.'

'The bank manager said he'd confirm in writing that my account was going to be transferred to his branch. Can you put it on the mantelpiece, I'll read it later.'

Joan suggested Hannah go out. 'Go and see your friends, take your mind off things. I expect Mary will make you a cup of tea.'

For some reason she didn't tell Joan she was going to the base as well as visiting Pond Farm. 'I'll be back before dark. Did you see all the mice Sooty killed for you?'

'I did and I reckon in a day or two we can let him out and he'll finish off the rats. I shouldn't bother to set traps, ducks, much better to let my clever cat do it for us.'

The day was cold and damp with a biting east wind, typical November weather and it suited her mood. Someone had told her there was nothing between Suffolk and Siberia and that the wind came from the frozen steppes straight to them. No wonder it was perishing.

The base was in roughly the same direction as the farm so there wasn't much of a detour. She was puffed by the time she'd pedalled up the hill and arrived at the main gate of the base. A flag hung at half-mast and the two men on guard duty looked suitably sombre.

She parked her bicycle and walked nervously to the gate. 'Excuse me, Flt Lt Rhodes has been staying at the same digs as me, he forgot this when he left this morning. Please could you make sure he gets it when he gets back from the funeral? It's very important.'

The younger of the two shouldered his rifle and greeted her with a friendly smile. 'Give it to us, love, I'll make sure he gets it.'

The envelope changed hands. 'Did everyone get back safely last night?'

'It weren't an op, love, just training. Nothing to worry about.'

Relieved there'd been no further casualties she smiled and cycled away. Did this mean there would be a sortie tonight instead? Jack wasn't well enough to fly. Dr Donnelly wouldn't let him until his stitches were removed. She mustn't worry about it; she had more pressing problems when she returned to the pub.

The police would want to talk to her; she didn't know what to tell them that wouldn't incriminate her. Why hadn't she spoken to Jack before he left? They should have the same story. What had he told them about the haversack? Had they even noticed it? Maybe they wouldn't speak to her separately; after all, to them Kurt was just one less German.

The ride to the farm cleared her head. She'd give Betty and Ruby an edited version of events. What on earth was she going to say? She was on the verge of turning round when a headscarf flew over the hedge. She recognized the scrap of orange cloth as Betty's.

She dropped her cycle and chased the material eventually trapping it under her shoe. She shook off the worst of the mud, walked to the five barred gate and climbed up to stare across the field of cabbages. She waved the orange square above her head. The two crouched figures straightened and waved back.

A thoroughly miserable looking horse stood between the shafts of the cart. The old blanket thrown over his withers flapped in the wind. There was no point in shouting; her words would be whipped away. She gestured towards the farm and the girls gave her a thumbs up. The cart was almost full, they must have been working since dawn to have picked so many. Daphne would be in the milking parlour which was the best place to be even if it did mean getting up at dawn.

She arrived at the farmyard to find Mr Boothroyd stomping about looking his usual disgruntled self. He scowled at her. 'I hope you ain't come here to stop my girls working, don't take to visitors on me farm. That's what you are now, Daphne's got your place, she moved her things in yesterday. You'll have to find somewhere else to go when your arm's better.'

'I see. I don't blame you, Mr Boothroyd. It will be several weeks before I can return, and I won't be able to do heavy work. I'll find somewhere else as soon as I'm better.'

He muttered and shambled across to the barn. She wasn't welcome here - should she wait for the girls or go home? Whilst the old misery was in the barn she'd speak to Mrs B, she wouldn't have heard what happened last night and even *he* would want to hear the news.

The farmhouse door opened as she approached. The kitchen windows faced the yard. 'Come along in, Hannah, don't take any notice of him. You're always welcome here; you come and see the girls any time you want.'

She left her shoes on the doormat and followed Mrs B. through the freezing house in to the welcome warmth of the kitchen. 'Betty and Ruby are on their way back, I expect they'll unload the cart before they stop for a drink. I was going to go across to the cottage and make them a cup of tea but I can't do that now I don't live there.'

'That Daphne's a nice girl, not a patch on you mind, but

she's a hard worker and gets on with old Arthur. She'll make them a cuppa, but you can pop across before you leave and say hello.' As Mrs B. was talking she'd pushed a large marmalade cat from the armchair by the fire. 'Sit here, then tell me how that Sooty has settled in.'

Hannah dropped her jacket over the back of the chair and sat down not sure how to start. 'Actually, I came to tell you something rather dreadful.' Mrs B. paused, the kettle poised over the tea pot. 'Jack and I went out for a walk last night, I know it sounds silly, but Joan doesn't like us ... well you know what I mean.' Her cheeks were scarlet - she was a rotten liar.

'Bit chilly for courting, but I don't blame you. It's the funeral today, isn't it? You never know what's going to happen; you make the most of things whilst you've got the chance. Nobody will blame you; folks understand how you young people feel.'

'Well, we ended up at the derelict cottages and were confronted by that German everyone's been looking for. Jack had his revolver with him. It wasn't me he wanted to be with. I was just an excuse for him to search for the pilot.' Her throat clogged, she swallowed but couldn't continue.

'Here, Hannah love, drink your tea. Tell me when you're feeling better.'

'Oh, Mrs Boothroyd, Jack killed him. The poor German, he didn't have a chance.' She scrambled for a handkerchief in her jacket pocket so she could turn away and hide her shame at having to lie.

'Well go to the foot of our stairs! Jack Rhodes shot him? I can hardly credit it. He seemed like such a nice, gentle young man. Just goes to show war changes folk.' She sat down heavily in one of the wooden chairs and rubbed her eyes on her apron. 'My Bert wasn't always like this—when our boy was lost at Dunkirk it changed him. I sank in to myself, let him bully me. But things are going to be different around here in future. I'm hoping Bert will move on too, but I'm not holding my breath.' She took a swig of tea. 'I daren't antagonise him, he's got handy with his fists.'

Hannah was unsurprised by this admission. Violence against anyone wasn't right. 'Don't let him hit you, Mrs B. He's no taller than you. Why not threaten him with a frying pan? A good bang on the head should stop his nonsense.'

Mrs Boothroyd laughed. 'You might be right, my dear. I'll try talking to him and if that doesn't work it's a frying pan. I expect you and Jack had words about it.'

'He's gone back to the base and I'm not seeing him again. I liked him but now I can't come back here I can look for something further away. Then he can still drink in his local, Joan will forgive him soon enough if I'm not there to remind her.'

'I hope you don't go too soon, you'll be missed round here. Ah, that's the cart. Give the girls three-quarters of an hour and then nip across whilst his nibs is in the barn.'

'Are you sure you want me to stay so long? I don't want to be in the way.'

'I want to hear about that cat, you picked the best of the bunch in my opinion. He was often around the back door mewing for scraps.'

*

The girls were suitably shocked when she gave them an edited version of what she'd told Mrs Boothroyd.

'Bleedin' Nora! I'd never put Jack down as a killer, some of the others what come in the pub, yes, but him?' Betty gave her muddy headscarf a final shake before tying it back. 'How do you feel about him now, Hannah?'

'It's over, he understands that. He's moved out and as I'll be leaving the area myself soon, it's for the best.'

'Don't throw the baby out with the bathwater,' Betty said.

'Think how many innocent people Jack and his mates have killed during this war? Bombs don't just kill bad people do they?'

'I know that; but this was different. Even though the German had a gun...'

'A gun? You never said he was armed. Course Jack had to shoot him. I would have done if some Nazi was pointing one at me.'

Hannah couldn't say any more, she'd said too much already. 'I hope you're comfortable in that little room, Daphne.'

Daphne patted her on the back. 'I am, beats sharing with half a dozen other girls. Sorry about taking your room, Hannah, but the cycling was just about killing me. You don't have to find somewhere else, Mrs What's-her-name, the posh lady who runs things around here, knows I'm happy to go back to working in a team when you're fit.'

'I don't mind. It's not fair on any of you the way things have been. Anyway, I'll have plenty of money once my account's transferred. I'll be a lady of leisure for the next few weeks. I'm going to join the WRVS, I can pack Red Cross parcels, take things to the post office and make cups of tea, even if I can't knit balaclavas.'

Ruby drained her mug and stood up. 'We'd better get back to the barn, old misery guts will be after us if we spend any longer here. Don't forget the social in the Village Hall this Saturday night. Not a dance exactly, although we have a knees-up after the party games and the beetle drive.'

'I shall definitely come, I've never been to a beetle drive.' She shivered theatrically. 'I take it real insects have nothing to do with this game?'

'Blimey, where've have you been all your life? Bit like bingo really.'

'I think everyone will need cheering up after today.'

Whilst returning to Debfield several fighters took off and

landed, these made her think about the funeral. Although she hoped Jack didn't do further damage to his shoulder, if he did he wouldn't be able to fly. She pedalled harder, pushing away her distress with each thrust of her feet. The girls had made her think. Jack couldn't have known Kurt wasn't going to pull the trigger. What he did was instinctive, what anyone else would have done.

She wobbled to a halt. Those awful things she had said to him - calling him a murderer. She was the one at fault, she'd been harbouring an enemy; all he'd done was his duty. The wind whipped her tears away as she puffed up the hill. She'd lost Jack but was still glad she'd helped Kurt. If only… too late for all that. Kurt was dead and this would always be a reminder to both of them.

*

Jack and the other chaps who were to be pallbearers opted to sit alongside the two flagdraped coffins in the back of the lorry. It was a bumpy and unpleasant ride to Cambridge. He'd not had time to speak to Hugh or the Wing Co about going back to active duty tonight, it would have to wait.

The lorry ground to a halt at the gates to the cemetery. He scrambled out and, alongside the other eleven men, straightened his greatcoat and put on his flat cap. The coffins were already resting on what looked like an enormous wooden stretcher. This had to be rolled from the lorry onto the long trailer that had been towed behind them, then six men would march on either side of it. At least he didn't have to bear the weight on his bad shoulder. Dave and Pete were not to be separated even in death. None of their relatives would be attending, it was to be a military affair.

As their commanding officer he took pole position on the left hand side, the others took their places and the lorry crawled forward. He'd attended a couple of funerals here before, it was a long trek to the grave, with each heavy step he felt the weight of his grief pressing him down.

The cortege slow marched down the gravel path, thirty or so men in double file behind them. Eventually they reached the two deep holes, side by side, mounds of freshly dug earth piled up to one side. The padre led the short interment service, Jack was glad no relatives were there to see how brief the ceremony was. Most of them had been to too many funerals, better to keep it brief and dignified.

Now he led men forward, they gripped the straps and gently lowered Pete in to the black hole. The other six simultaneously laid Dave to rest. They stood, heads bowed whilst the rifles fired a final salute and it was done. On his command they about turned and marched swiftly back to the waiting bus.

He didn't want to speak to anyone, the blokes respected his silence but the bus was noisy, full of tobacco smoke and loud laughter. He'd seen it all before, once the funeral was over those left behind moved on. New aircrew would arrive to fill the spaces, like dropping a stone in to the pond once the ripples vanished it was as though the dead men had never existed.

He closed his eyes and rested his damp cheek against the window, it had to be that way. No-one could fly night after night if they continued to grieve for those that had died. Live in the present, that's the only way you

could stay sane. The boys would all get drunk, drown their sorrows in warm beer. He'd go to the officers' mess and do the same. For him this was a double tragedy, he'd lost his best friends and the girl he loved.

On reaching the base the bus screeched to a halt and everyone piled out. He headed straight to their medical centre. Hugh was writing up his notes in the office. 'Can you take out my stitches, Hugh, and give me the all clear? I want to get back in the air ASAP.'

'Come in to the surgery, I'll have a look at your shoulder. Stitches usually stay in for a week, it's only been five days for yours.'

'It doesn't hurt at all, my head's as clear as a bell, I need to be working again. Take my mind off things.'

Twenty minutes later he had his medical discharge, with this clutched firmly in one hand he strode to the Wing Commander's office. Gerald stood up and shook his hand.

'Just the man, I heard you were back on the base. Is that for me?' He held out his hand and Jack handed over the slip of paper Hugh had given him. 'Excellent. I've found us another crate, but someone's going to have to go and get it. It's one that landed in Kent, it's fully repaired and ready for collection.'

'I'll go if you want.'

'Good show. You can go first thing tomorrow, you'll be needed tonight.'

'With any luck I can hitch a ride most of the way. Do I get a travel docket?'

The Wing Co waved his arm at a pile of papers spilling off the edge of his cluttered desk. 'Help yourself, old man, fill in the details. You'd better stamp it before you leave. I'll give the base at tinkle and let them know you're coming.'

Smiling Jack left the office, paperwork was not Stanton's priority. He bumped in to Johnny Page, his squadron leader, on the way out.

'Heard you were back, Jack. Good man. A big op on tonight, briefing in two hours. Glad to have you on board. Not looking forward to this op - Dresden's a bugger.'

Jack returned to his rooms to change in to his flying jacket and boots, he wasn't sure whose plane he'd be flying, or who his crew would be. Not to worry, he'd find out soon enough. There must be a pilot on the sick list and he was needed to take his place. He didn't like flying other people's kites, every plane had its own idiosyncrasies and there was only a fraction of a second to make the right decision or the wrong one.

He patted his jacket pocket. The hair on the back of his neck stood up. Why the hell had he given back his lucky talisman?

Chapter Sixteen

Hannah parked her bike in the shed in the dark. She was exhausted, had overdone it, but at least she'd sleep tonight. The back door was flung open as she raised her hand to lift the latch.

'Here you are last, the police came round and you'll never guess what they said.'

'That they'll be back to see me tomorrow morning?' She carried her gumboots in to the scullery, pushed her feet in to her slippers and hung up her jacket. The cat purred around her legs, his warmth steadying her.

'Sit, ducks, have a cuppa whilst I tell you.' Joan handed her a steaming enamel mug and Sooty leapt nimbly in to her lap and curled up. 'He's been watching the door all day; I reckon he's got a soft spot for you as well.'

'What did the police say, Joan?'

'They said the Nazi pilot isn't dead. He banged his head when he fell and that's why everyone thought he was a goner. They're keeping him in hospital another day and then he'll be shipped to a P O W camp somewhere up north.'

The scalding liquid slopped onto the table. 'Not dead? I can't believe it, there was so much blood and he was deathly pale.' She couldn't continue. Joan removed the tea from her hand.

'There, I should have realised it'd be a shock.'

Hannah closed her eyes. Jack wasn't a killer, whatever his intentions when he'd pulled the trigger, he didn't have an innocent man's death on his conscience. Whatever happened between Jack and her, Kurt was safe. These past few days had not been wasted.

'I'm fine now. I can't tell you how pleased I am Jack's not a murderer. Does that mean the police won't speak to me?'

'It does. They'll call in at the base, I expect, to speak to Flt Lt Rhodes, but that's not your concern, is it, dear?'

Now would not be a good time to tell Joan about the trip to the base. One thing she'd learnt about her landlady was she was quick to anger but equally quick to forgive. In a few days Jack would be able to come in to the pub if he wanted to.

When, at six o'clock, the roar of planes taking off made conversation impossible Hannah sent out a fervent prayer they would return safely. Jack would be flying an unfamiliar aircraft with crew he didn't know, but at least he had his lucky charms. He'd return safely, he had to.

*

The White Hart was packed by seven thirty. Hannah found pouring drinks difficult but had mastered tray carrying and was busy taking drinks and clearing tables. The lack of aircrew amongst the drinkers was something no one referred to. The conversations seemed mostly to be about the German pilot, for some reason nobody associated her with his capture.

Towards the end of the evening a smiling young man tapped on the shoulder. 'Here, miss, you're the young lady what brought the letter for Flt Lt Rhodes ain't you?'

She paused, a tray full of dirty glasses balanced precariously on her plaster cast. 'I am, and you're the young man

169

who offered to see it reached him. You've not been here before have you?'

'No, I ain't. Just bin posted here, finding me feet, if you know what I mean.'

'We serve the best beer. By the way, did my letter reach Flt Lt Rhodes?'

His jaunty expression faded. 'I'm sorry, miss, but I forgot about it until this afternoon. I couldn't go in the briefing, I give it to one of the blokes what looks after his quarters and he promised to do it. He'll find it there when he gets back from the op.'

The tray wobbled and disaster was averted by a WAAF. 'Gosh, that was close. Let me take it for you, you don't look too clever.'

Hannah pushed her way through the sweating crowd and in to the comparative calm of the saloon bar. There were a few locals playing dominoes, they grunted a greeting and returned to their game.

Her heart was pounding; she gripped the back of a chair taking several deep breaths until her vision cleared. She was being ridiculous. Everyone knew having photographs and things in a pocket for good luck was superstition - it wouldn't make the slightest difference to Jack if he flew without his talismans. The girl with the tray arrived beside her.

'I'll take these through for you. Hannah, isn't it? I'm Beverley, everyone calls me Bev.'

'Thank you, Bev, I've been overdoing it. What with all the excitement last night, then I went for a very long bike ride today and now this.'

'If you'll show me where to put these you can have a breather. I'll collect glasses until you feel better.'

Hannah didn't want Joan to know she was upset. Jack was supposed to be out of her life but everything had changed because Kurt wasn't dead. 'I'm okay now; the glasses go in the scullery, thanks. There's a tray full you could bring back for me if you don't mind.'

By nine thirty Hannah was flagging. The locals had gone home and only a dozen RAF personnel remained. 'Joan, do you mind if I go up? I'll clear the bar when I get up tomorrow.'

'Gracious, of course you can, ducks. You look a bit peaky, I must say. Don't suppose you got much sleep last night. Off you go, don't worry, you get up when you feel like it. You've done more than enough tonight.'

'Thanks. I'm going then. Goodnight.'

She had so much to think about. Things might change; if she and Jack put the past behind them she wouldn't move away and maybe she could replace Daphne and work as part of a team.

With her hot water bottle tucked under her arm she braved the chilly upstairs corridor. Certain she wouldn't sleep until she'd counted the planes in she snuggled under the blankets and eiderdown. She woke when her door opened the following morning and Joan appeared carrying a cup of tea.

'Here you are, ducks, lady of leisure this morning. It's perishing in here, stay where you are and I'll get the fire going.'

'Good grief, it's almost nine o'clock; I've been asleep for hours. I intended to stay awake until the boys got back. Did you hear them return, Joan?'

'No, I sleep right through nowadays. Sit up, drink your tea whilst it's hot. See, it's in a cup and saucer this morning, and there's a couple of ginger nuts as well.'

'Thank you, what a lovely surprise. I can't remember ever having a cup of tea in bed before, not even when I had measles years ago.'

Joan handed over the drink and then got down on her hands and knees to clear the grate and lay the fire. 'Well, it's high time somebody spoilt you then. Don't hurry down, I've finished the chores.' She struck a match against the bricks and lit the newspaper under the kindling. 'There, be nice and cosy in here in a minute. You'll never guess what I found this morning.'

Hannah laughed. 'I bet I can - a pile of dead rats.'

'That bloomin' cat's a miracle. I've got rid of the dirt tray, his nibs lets himself in and out.'

Joan left her to enjoy her tea. Hannah decided to go to Saffron Walden and get some money to buy Joan and her friends presents. There were still loads of coupons in her ration book; there must be something she could exchange those for.

An image of Giles filled her mind - he was the only one she'd exchanged gifts with at Christmas and birthdays. This year would be different as she had friends as well as Joan (who was more like a relative now). Would she have a young man to select a gift for?

She was dressed and in the kitchen by ten o'clock. 'I thought I might go in to town, Joan, is there anything you want?'

'There's lots of things I'd like but little chance of you buying them. A lovely bit of lavender soap, some talc, a pair of stockings … but I'll manage with what I've got as usual.'

Sooty turned towards the door his tail erect. Hannah raised her eyebrows and heard the sound of footsteps approaching. She was on her way when the knock came. Mrs Boothroyd was shifting from foot to foot outside the door.

'I hope I'm not intruding, I was in the village and thought I'd pop in.'

Joan rushed forward beaming widely. 'Mary, what a lovely surprise. Come along in, we're just having elevenses.'

Hannah took Mrs B's coat and gloves but their visitor kept her hat on. 'I'm glad you've called in Mrs B. I'll do the tea for you if you like, Joan.'

'I've come to see how the cat settled. Do you have him shut in somewhere?'

The scullery window banged and Sooty rushed in bearing a gift. Proudly he dropped a large rabbit at Joan's feet. The animal's eyes were glazed but its sides were heaving. 'Quickly, grab the cat. The rabbit's still alive.'

Joan scooped Sooty up and carried him in to the scullery and closed the door. 'I'll break its neck for you; it'll make a lovely meal.' Joan lent down.

'No, I'm going to put it outside. If it dies then I won't mind eating it, but not if *you* kill it.'

Rabbits were flea infested and also had sharp claws. She grabbed an old tablecloth and wrapped the rabbit up. Forgetting she was in her slippers she ran to the bottom of the garden and emptied the the animal under the hedge. 'There, I can't do anything else for you. It's up to you now.'

When she returned Joan was sitting at the table with the cat curled up in her lap. Both women shook their heads.

'You'll never make a country girl, ducks, not with your soft heart. Fancy letting a lovely fat rabbit get away.'

'Sorry, I couldn't help myself. There's been too much death in the village already.' Unrepentant she kicked off her wet slippers and joined them in her socks. 'Has Joan told you about the German pilot, Mrs B?'

'She has, not sure if I'm pleased or not. Still, it's less of a palaver for Jack this way.'

Hannah desperately wanted to tell them Kurt hadn't gunned down Pete and Dave but the only person she'd explain this to was Jack . Tomorrow she'd persuade Joan to let him back - that's if he wanted to come.

Their guest departed too late for Hannah to catch the bus. Whilst Joan put her feet up and got out her knitting Hannah started on the mountain of ironing. A lot of the laundry was still damp but it ironed better that way and there was less chance of scorching the material with the hot flat-irons.

'Put the wireless on, ducks, I think it's time for Tommy Handley.'

Hannah went to check if the rabbit had recovered. She shone her torch and sighed at the stiffened corpse. It would have been kinder to let Mrs B. finish it off and not leave it to die in pain.

Joan appeared behind her. 'Let me take it, ducks, I don't want you upsetting yourself again.'

Hannah sniffed. 'I'll skin it for you, if you want. I've done it several times, I don't mind if the rabbit arrives already cold.'

'No, not to worry, it won't take me a jiffy. I can cook up what we won't use for pussy. He deserves a share.' Joan grabbed the rabbit by the hind feet and vanished in to the gloom swinging it at her side.

Hannah wasn't sure she'd be able to eat it. But with meat in short supply and everything rationed, having a whole rabbit was a luxury. She'd been horribly sick each time she'd had to kill a chicken for the pot; Joan was right, she wasn't cut out to be a farm girl.

*

That evening the pub was heaving with aircrew. No one had mentioned any losses; she'd been worrying unnecessarily about Jack.

The young man from last night was there. He greeted her enthusiastically. 'Nice to see you, miss, I've brought me mate along tonight. He's an officer's servant, the one what looks after that flight lieutenant of yours.'

'Good to meet you.' She smiled and was about to turn away when something prompted her to ask, 'Flt Lt Rhodes, is he likely to be coming in tonight do you know?'

The bespectacled boy, for he looked scarcely old enough to be called a man, shook his head. 'He's not been back to his rooms since yesterday. His kit bag's where he left it yesterday, took me bleedin' ages to put everything back in the drawers.'

Hannah's world tilted. Voices faded. Jack had been shot down. He'd flown without her lock of hair and photograph and his luck had run out last night. She had to get away, be on her own. She elbowed her way through the packed bar not caring if people saw her. The man she loved was lost. Her life was over.

*

Jack staggered out of the Blenheim; by his reckoning he'd been awake for more than forty-eight hours and it was a miracle he'd found Debfield in the darkness. A couple of ground crew were waiting to give the new crate the once over.

'Flies like a dream, a lot sharper than the old one. I'm off to my pit; I need some shut eye.'

'I'll let Wing Co know you're here, sir. He'll be pleased you're back in one piece.'

'I managed a bit of a kip on the train, thank God. Nothing planned for tonight I hope?'

'No, sir, most of them are down the pub or in the mess.'

He was too knackered to go to either place. He dozed as the driver bounced across the runway onto the perimeter but was jolted fully awake when the vehicle screeched to a halt outside his quarters.

Inside was quiet. He glanced at his watch; he'd made good time from Kent, it wasn't quite eight o'clock. It took him three attempts to get the key in but eventually he pushed open the door. When he switched the light on the first thing he saw was a white envelope propped on the mantelpiece.

He'd better read it, probably bad news from home. Funny, he didn't recognize the writing and there was no stamp on it. Something had been scribbled on the back in pencil. This was the time and date it arrived at the base. Crikey - it had been here since Monday morning. Tearing open the envelope he pulled out a single sheet of paper and something dropped onto the floor.

His eyes widened. It was Hannah's lock of hair and photograph. Why had she sent these back to him? He scanned the brief note and his fatigue vanished. She'd written this before she could have known the German had survived. If she could forgive him then he must do the same for her.

Stuffing the letter and talismans in to his inside pocket he headed for the door. He couldn't risk cycling, he'd end up in a ditch. He'd requisition a vehicle. No one else would land tonight so he could safely take a jeep without it being missed. The drivers usually parked them outside their billets; all he had to do was stroll around until he found one.

When he roared through the gates ten minutes later the two men on duty barely had time to step aside. Five minutes later he was outside the pub. It didn't matter what Joan thought, Hannah was all that mattered.

He reeled back as the noise and smoke filled atmosphere overwhelmed him. His height meant he could see over most heads and he spotted Hannah straightaway. She was talking to a young man he'd never seen before. He shouldered his way through the press, was about to call out when something the bloke said changed everything.

Her colour drained, her hands flew to her mouth and she turned and ran through the bar. He'd flatten the blighter for upsetting her. In two strides he was there and gripped the man's shoulder spinning him round.

'What did you say to her?'

The man's eyes widened and he swallowed. 'Nothing, sir, she asked if you were coming and I told her you hadn't been in your rooms, that nobody had seen you today. Then she went all peculiar and ran off.'

'Hell and blast! She thinks I went for a burton. Not your fault.'

Ignoring the complaints from those he pushed aside he followed her; he could hear her crying as he reached the head of the stairs.

*

Curled up in a ball Hannah pressed her face in to the pillow trying to muffle her sobs. Nothing had prepared her for the pain of losing Jack; even Giles going missing hadn't been as bad. A cold draught made her shiver. She ought to get under the covers.

Suddenly she was lifted from the bed and enveloped in his arms. 'It's all right, darling, I'm here. You misunderstood, don't cry like that, it'll make you ill.'

Choking back her tears she buried her face in his shoulder hardly able to believe he was beside her. 'You didn't have your lucky charms, that man told me you hadn't collected them.' She gulped and wiped her nose on his shirt. 'Then, when he said no one had seen you, I just thought …'

'I know, sweetheart, I'm sorry. You've been through enough lately without this.'

She pushed herself away, tracing the outline of his face, too overcome, too happy, to ask where he'd been. 'I must take my shoes off; I can't be bothered to undress. Don't leave me; hold me for a bit longer, I still can't believe you're here.'

'I'm not going anywhere; I'm back in your life for good. Explanations can wait until tomorrow.'

By the light of his torch she unlaced her shoes and dropped them onto the rag rug, his boots followed. Good grief! They shouldn't be in her bedroom, Joan would have something to say about it when she found out. She must tell him to go. But not for a few minutes, she needed the comfort of his arms for a while.

'Jack, you can't stay too long, you know what Joan's like.'

'Tonight's different, we need each other. She'll understand. Anyway, I'll be gone long before she comes up, she'll never know.'

He propped himself against the wall and she settled in to his arms, he pulled the eiderdown across them. She could feel his heart thumping, hear him breathing - she'd never felt more at peace. She relaxed and the fear and anxiety of the past ten days evaporated. When she told him why she'd helped the German he'd understand. They mustn't get too comfortable; he'd have to leave in a minute.

'Jack, you must go.' He didn't answer. The torch was resting on the edge of the bed; she flicked it on and shone the beam on his face. There were deep lines etched down either side of his mouth, oil and grime embedded in the skin - he'd not even washed before he came rushing out. Then she noticed he was wearing the uniform he flew in, his leather jacket and big boots lay on the floor.

He looked so tired she hadn't the heart to wake him. With a sigh she snuggled back on to his chest and his arm slid around her waist drawing her closer. Heaven knows what would happen tomorrow but tonight she didn't care.

Chapter Seventeen

The blackout curtains were drawn and there was no sign of her sleeping companion when Hannah opened her eyes. She'd overslept for the second time and had no idea when Jack had woken and left. As she stripped off her rumpled clothes she noticed he'd written her a note on the back of the letter she'd given him.

Darling girl,

Thank God I woke up in time to spare both our blushes. If I hadn't got the jeep back to base before dawn I'd have been up on a charge. I'm going to be busy the next few days getting to know my crew and we've got to do a couple of training runs in the new Blenheim I went to fetch yesterday.

I love you, whatever's happened between us, let's put it in the past.

I don't know when I'll be in again, but I'll definitely be there for the social on Saturday.

I want to wake up every morning to find you sleeping in my arms.

Yours for ever
Jack

Golly, he felt the same way she did. She read it again and then folded the paper and slipped it under her pillow. This was her first love letter and she'd treasure it for ever. Presumably he'd escaped without alerting Joan. With some trepidation she approached the kitchen where she could hear Joan talking to the cat. She needn't have worried—her landlady greeted her with her usual cheery smile.

'Morning, ducks. You looked so comfortable I didn't like to wake you this morning. Bev said you were upset about something. Is that why you slept in your clothes?'

'I thought Jack had died; someone from the base told me he hadn't been seen since the sortie and his bed hadn't been slept in.' Joan was looking bewildered. 'When I saw he'd left his lucky charms behind I had to take them to him. And then when we heard the German pilot was going to be all right... well... it all clicked back in to place.'

'Fair enough. People do funny things in the heat of the moment. If you love him, that's good enough for me. Was he here last night? I never saw him.'

'He arrived just as I heard what I thought was news of his death, he followed me up to my room and we sorted everything out before he went home.' She bent down to scratch Sooty hoping to hide her pink cheeks. She held her breath waiting for Joan to ask the question.

'So everything's ticketyboo? Did he tell you where he'd been?'

'He'd been to fetch a plane to replace the Blenheim he crashed last week. Anyway, he's going to be training his new crew, but he'll be here for the Saturday social.'

Joan nodded. 'Had to be something like that, you were daft to think he'd had it. Don't you think one of the other blokes would have known?'

'I was silly but I was wound up so it's hardly surprising I got it wrong. Now, is there anything you want me to do this morning?'

'Can you do the rabbit? I've still got a bit of lard and enough flour for pastry if you want to make a pie.'

Hannah didn't want to make anything with the wretched animal. She forced her mouth to curve. 'I could make a tasty casserole, we've plenty of the vegetables. I can't manage pastry with a cast.'

'Sounds lovely. I'm going to the WRVS meeting later; you want to come with me?'

'I do, as I'm no longer in the Land Army I've got to do my bit for the war effort. If I get a move on I can catch the midday bus.'

Her trip to Saffron Walden was uneventful. As expected her account was active and she withdrew £25 - plenty for the gifts she wanted and enough to pay her board and lodging for a few weeks.

Joan was dismayed when she suggested putting their arrangement on a financial footing. 'I don't want your money. I think of you like my own flesh and blood, if you start paying me it won't be the same.'

'Please let me contribute to the housekeeping. Even a family member would chip in when they could afford it wouldn't they?' Hannah gave Joan the two small bars of lily of the valley scented soap she'd bought on her shopping trip. 'I got these for you as a thank you for making me so welcome.'

'Bless you, you shouldn't have. Don't spend your pennies on me, my girl, I've a feeling you're going to need to start filling your bottom drawer.'

'It's too soon to be talking about that; we've not known each other long enough. Maybe after Christmas?' She put the presents for her friends on the table. 'I wanted to get them all stockings but didn't have enough coupons. Do you think they'll be happy with bath salts?'

'They will - you're a generous girl, I count it a lucky day when you moved in.'

Hannah smiled ruefully. 'If someone had asked me three weeks ago if breaking my arm was a good option I'd have laughed. Yet here I am warm and comfortable, living with you and not having to go outside in this horrible weather *and* I'm in love with a wonderful man.'

The clatter of the scullery window closing behind the cat made her stiffen dreading what he might have got this time. Joan had removed three dead rats from the kitchen already.

'Golly, another rabbit. Excuse me; I feel a pressing need to tidy something upstairs.' Joan's laughter followed her upstairs. At this rate they would be able to supply the whole village with fresh meat.

*

The remainder of the week passed quickly, Hannah no longer asked what she could do but just got on with it. Joan was becoming the mother she'd never known. Sooty continued to bring in the occasional rat and two more plump rabbits appeared as well. When the butcher's van came round on Friday morning Hannah bartered these for a decent sized joint of beef, a pound of sausages and a tub of beef dripping.

'There's enough for a feast here, love, why don't you ask Jack to join us on Sunday? He could stay Saturday night if he doesn't have to be back for church parade.'

Hannah hugged Joan. 'Thank you, what a lovely idea. I'll cycle out there with a note. Can I ask the girls as well? They could bring vegetables and half a dozen eggs to make a Yorkshire pudding.'

'Go on then, it'll be a real treat sitting down with a full table on Sunday. I've got plenty of apples stored in the pantry, I'll make a pie for afters.'

*

Saturday evening eventually arrived. Hannah was wearing the same frock she'd worn the night she met Jack which seemed appropriate somehow. He'd sent a message accepting the invitation and promising to be at the pub by opening time. His room was ready, the fire laid, the bed freshly changed. She'd even taken clean water for him to wash tomorrow morning. Joan suggested she tip some in to a metal jug and stand it in the fireplace so he had warm water for his shave.

She checked her lipstick wasn't smudged, her unruly hair was securely pinned in its French pleat, that her stocking seams were straight and then she was ready. Joan had asked a couple of friends to help in the bar so she'd have the whole evening free to enjoy herself.

Where was her torch? She was going to need it when they went to the village hall. She checked her dressing table and then remembered she'd left it in the pocket of the coat which was hanging in the scullery.

There was the sound of voices, both male and female, and the clatter of bicycles being dropped outside. If she didn't hurry she wouldn't be in the bar to greet her friends when they came in.

She was keeping the surprises for tomorrow; she hoped they *would* be able to come to lunch. The butcher had agreed to take her invitation to the farm as he was calling in to collect a side of bacon on his way home.

She gave the cat a wide berth, she didn't want him laddering her precious stockings as these were her last pair. The fire in the saloon bar was crackling merrily because Joan expected the locals to come across for a nightcap after the social. This being a family event it finished much earlier than a dance.

Already customers were threading their way through the blackout curtains but Jack wasn't among them and neither were the girls. She knew most of them and was soon absorbed in to their group but each time the door latch rattled she turned.

'Crikey, he must be something special the way you're watching the door,' Bev said. 'I hope he's worth it.'

Hannah's smile was radiant. 'He is, and I've not seen him since Tuesday. My friends from the farm have arrived, please excuse me, I've not seen them for ages either.'

Betty rushed forward her arms outstretched and gave her a smacking kiss. 'You're a dark horse, then. Fancy getting engaged to that Jack and not telling your best friends.'

Hannah's smile slipped. 'Where did you hear that? It's certainly not true, we've made up but we're not engaged.'

'Mrs B. got it from the husband of a friend who was there when the German was shot. Jack told the bobby you were his fiancée.'

'I expect he was trying to make it look less shocking we were out in the middle of the night together. It's the first I've heard of it anyway. Please, don't say anything to him when he comes.'

Ruby and Daphne were waiting to embrace her too. She'd never had so many kisses in one day.

'I'm not re-joining the Land Army, I've joined the WRVS instead and I'm going on a first aid course when my arm's mended and maybe, if I take to it, I'll train as a nurse. I'm also on fire watch and I thought I might join the Home Guard.'

This was greeted by hoots of laughter. Ruby wiped her eyes. 'I shouldn't bother until Captain Turner retires - imagine having him bossing you about, far worse than old Boothroyd.'

Why wasn't Jack here? Her excitement seeped away; the evening wouldn't be the same without him. Whatever was keeping him this time? She looked around the bar. 'Betty, none of Jack's squadron is here. Can you see anybody you know?'

All three girls stared around the room checking for familiar faces amongst a crowd of grey blue uniforms. Daphne shook her head. 'You're right, Hannah, there must be a flap on. I don't suppose any of them will come tonight.'

*

At the base Jack finished his inspection of the new Blenheim. 'What do you think you two? Ready to go whenever?' he asked as he dropped to the concrete. 'It's bloody cramped, but everything works and it's a damned sight more manoeuvrable than some others I've flown.'

Pilot Officer George Reynolds who was his navigator, peeled back the earmuffs on his flying helmet and ruffled his ginger hair. 'I've heard blokes call the Beaufort 'the flying coffin' because it's so difficult to get out of in an emergency. At least the Blenheim doesn't have that reputation.'

The craggy face of the new rear gunner and bomb aimer, Flight Sergeant Cyril Smith, appeared behind them. 'Okay up my end, skipper. Can see for miles in the turret, no German bugger will get the better of me.'

'Good, you two coming down for the beetle drive? I went to the last one - after a few pints of beer it was bloody good fun.' The distinctive roar of an approaching aircraft drowned out their reply. He turned to stare through the darkness at the deserted runway. Someone in the tower must have picked up the incoming plane as one by one the lights came on.

Who the hell was this? As far as he knew none of the fighters were up, must be one of the female pilots delivering an urgent part. It was hard to distinguish the plane in the darkness but he could see it heading for the control tower. The cockpit slammed back and someone scrambled down on to the wing, dropped to the floor and ran to speak to the man who had emerged from the tower.

His head flew back, his hand dropped to his revolver.

The man was speaking in English. He, hotly pursued by his crew, haired towards what was obviously a German plane. The intruder, realising his mistake, hurtled back to his plane screaming something in German. The Messerschmitt, he could identify it easily now he was closer, began to taxi in a tight circle.

He raised his gun and fired - too late, the plane was out of range. 'Turn off the bloody lights, you imbeciles, he can't take off in the dark.'

Someone finally reacted and the runway was plunged in to darkness, but the plane completed his take off safely and roared away in to the night.

'I'll go to the foot of our stairs! Would you Adam and Eve it? A bloody Nazi landed on our airbase and got away.' Cyril dropped his helmet on the floor and stamped on it in disgust.

'It's too late to scramble the fighters, the bastard will be long gone by the time they get after him.' Jack felt like jumping on something too but restrained the impulse. Hugh Donnelly and a couple of other bods rolled up in a jeep.

'Was that a German? Couldn't believe my eyes when I saw the swastika,' Hugh said.

'I'd better go and report to the control tower, they must be reeling after that.' Jack had an irresistible desire to laugh and tried to swallow it unsuccessfully. 'Bloody hell, no one will believe what's just happened...' he choked, unable to continue, rocking from side to side his laughter booming across the empty space.

Soon the others joined in and when Stanton turned up five minutes later they were all incapable of speech, tears running down their faces. The Wing Co scowled at them, shrugged and marched off to give the blokes in the control tower a dressing down.

By the time Jack was ready to leave he was damned late. He daren't misappropriate a jeep tonight, he was already in bad odour for not taking the incident seriously and if he had to cycle he wouldn't be there until everyone had gone over to the village hall. Nothing for it, he'd have to be late and hope his unlikely explanation would be enough to smooth the matter over.

He was at the gate when a battered van pulled over and the window was wound down. 'Want a lift to the village, Jack, shove your bike in the back, I've only a few bits and pieces in there tonight.'

'Thanks, had a bit of a drama just as I was about to leave and it's made me late.' Jimmy found the incident as funny as he had; they were both still chuckling when he was dropped off outside The White Hart. A steady flow of people was already trickling from the front door, hopefully Hannah would still be inside.

*

The pub was emptying and still no sign of her escort. Hannah turned to her friends. 'Go on without me, Jack's bound to arrive soon and I'll come across with him.' The blackout curtain moved and he stepped in. She ran across the bar and launched herself in to his arms. He twirled her around like a child, laughing down at her.

He slid her down his front and every bit that touched him tingled deliciously. His eyes changed colour and before she could argue he tightened his grip; his mouth covered hers in a kiss that demanded a response. Her friends were laughing, saying they'd see her in the hall.

Joan intervened. 'Now then, Jack, put my girl down. Time and place for that sort of thing and it's not in my bar, I can tell you.'

Hannah's feet touched the boards but his arms stayed firmly about her waist. 'Sorry, Joan, got a bit carried away. Not seen the woman I love for far too long.'

Joan's expression softened, she smiled at them both. 'Never mind all that nonsense. If you don't get a move on the beetle drive will start without you.' She pointed to Hannah's mouth. 'Your lipstick's smudged, ducks, you'd better powder your nose before you leave. I'll give your young man a drink whilst you tidy yourself up.'

'You'll have to gulp it down, Jack, I won't be more than a minute and I'm definitely not missing the fun tonight.'

In the mirror above the mantelpiece she quickly repaired the damage and tucked in the stray curls that had come unpinned. Her cheeks were glowing; her eyes sparkled back at her. Nothing mattered, not the war, not Ralph Mayhew, not anything apart from her love for Jack. A happy future opened up in front of her; by some miracle she'd survived a miserable childhood, being raped and what could have been a permanent break-up with Jack.

He was draining the last of his pint when she got back. 'Now, Flt Lt Rhodes, kindly explain why you're so late tonight.'

'Let's forget about it, we've got tomorrow to talk. I warn you, I'm going to have to nip back to the pub for another beer, I'm way behind everyone else.'

*

The evening was like nothing she'd experienced before; she could imagine her stepmother's disdain if *she'd* been asked to attend this function. Jack dashed out twice to down a pint and he wasn't the only man to do so. When the party games started the crowd was more than a bit merry.

She wondered what the dozen or so children made of the antics of the inebriated adults but they seemed to take it in their stride. No doubt many of the parents were as giggly and silly as the RAF personnel.

After the last game of musical chairs she found time

to speak to the girls. 'Did you three get the invitation for lunch?'

'We did, Mr Misery Guts said no, but Mrs B. was having none of that. I don't know what you've done to her, Hannah, but she's a new woman. So we'll be with you at noon; it's nice of you to ask us. I can't remember when I last had a proper Sunday roast,' Ruby said.

'You should have seen his face, it was a picture wasn't it, Betty? Daphne was in the dairy, she missed the kerfuffle.'

After the games there were a couple of polkas, a waltz and a jitterbug and then the evening was over. The families departed their children overexcited and full of fairy cakes and orange squash. Everyone else was going to The Plough or The White Hart.

Jack had his arm round her waist; he staggered as the cold air hit him. 'It's a good thing I'm holding you up; you wouldn't get there under your own steam,' Hannah said.

Betty and Ruby were tipsy and larking about with a group of RAF playing some sort of tag. This wasn't sensible in the dark. The wavering light of their torches wouldn't keep them safe. Jack released her and stepped forward shouting a warning.

'Look out! You'll be in the pond in a minute. It's right behind you.'

The man chasing Betty didn't hear him. There was a ghastly crack of splintering wood, a hideous scream and an almighty splash.

Chapter Eighteen

'Good grief, not again. This is the fifth time this year; you'd think they'd learn. Get some blankets - I'll see if I can fish them out.'

Jack vanished in to the darkness and Hannah ran the remaining distance to the pub. People were milling about not sure whether to offer assistance or go in the warm and get themselves a stiff drink for the shock. Nobody seemed to be taking it seriously.

She pushed her way through and met Joan coming out. 'Here, ducks, I popped upstairs and brought down some old blankets. Whoever fell in the pond is going to need them, it's perishing tonight. Thank God the water's not deep. I've got Ada and Pam making hot water bottles and a big pot of tea.'

Hannah grabbed the armful and calling her thanks ran back towards the racket, hoping it wasn't anyone she knew. As she arrived at the pond Betty staggered to the edge. The airman who'd gone in with her put his shoulder under her backside and shoved her in to the waiting arms of Daphne and Ruby.

Jack loomed out of the darkness and she handed him one of the blankets. 'Great, you get Betty inside and I'll bring this idiot.'

Her friend was spitting muddy water on the road. 'Come

on; put this round you, Joan's getting everything ready.'

Betty could hardly speak through her shivers and clattering teeth. 'I've lost my bleedin' shoes in that bleedin' pond. I'll have to get them when I got my gumboots on.'

She dripped and swore as Hannah and the other two helped her squelch to the pub. The side door was open, wet customers weren't welcome in the bar. Joan greeted her unexpected guest briskly. 'In the scullery, get your clothes off young lady, there's towels to dry yourself and one of my old nighties and Hannah's dressing gown to put on. You'll have to be quick unless you want to undress in front of the airman.'

Joan had four hot water bottles ready. Heavy footsteps approached the kitchen door; Jack had brought the other victim. He told the man to strip to his underwear outside. Fortunately for Betty's dignity she was safely bundled up in dry things and huddling by the fire. Joan greeted the blanket clad, and somewhat shamefaced, young man with a friendly smile.

'Oh, I might have known it would be you, Fred Simpson, you ought to know better. This is the second time I've had to dry you out this year.'

He shuffled forward clutching his damp blanket around his embarrassment. 'Sorry, Joan, you know what it's like when you've had a few. It was worse this time, mud up to your armpits, they've been driving ambulances through the pond so Digger told me. Bleedin' stupid game, if you ask me.'

Jack came in with him but his mates disappeared down the path and in to the bar to have a few more drinks. 'God knows what you're going to put on, Fred; you'll have to go back to the base in a blanket.' He was having difficulty keeping a straight face.

'I've put some of my Bill's clothes out, Fred; you're half his size but they're better than nothing.' Joan put her hands on her hips and tried to look disapproving. 'If you're going to keep this up you'd better leave a spare set of clothes in my scullery.'

Betty couldn't stop shivering. Her teeth clattered on the rim of the mug and half the tea went down the dressing gown. Her hair straggled around her face and her eyes were bloodshot and sore. 'I think you'll be better off in bed, you're not well enough to cycle back. I lit the fire in Jack's room, you can go there, the sheets are fresh,' Joan said.

'Ta ever so, I don't feel too clever. Me stomach's all over the place, I reckon I swallowed half a gallon of pond water.'

'Not to worry, I'll make sure you've got a basin.'

Hannah looked at the other two hovering anxiously on either side of their bedraggled friend. 'Can you help Betty and I'll carry the lamp and hot water bottles.'

Leaving Ruby and Daphne to settle Betty she returned to the kitchen to find Jack alone. 'Has Fred gone back to the base already?'

'Not likely, he's in the bar getting a stiff drink. How's Betty?'

'She'll be okay; the others are going to stay until she goes to sleep, just in case. Is there any tea in that pot? I need a cup after all the excitement.'

There was no sign of the cat, too many strangers had obviously alarmed him. She sipped her tea thoughtfully. 'I can't imagine anywhere in the country having so much excitement. Is it always like this?'

He dragged his chair over so his knees touched hers. 'Always; we've had bombing raids, visits from royalty and George Formby came here to make a film.'

The feel of his legs was lovely, not threatening, just companionable and warm. She sighed but couldn't hold back her yawn. 'We still haven't talked about the other night. I've got to tell you…'

'You haven't. We've moved on, we both did things we

regret…'

'Hang on a minute, who says I regret anything? *You* tried to kill someone. I helped him, protected him. *I've* got nothing to be ashamed of.' She was wide awake and glared at him, daring him to disagree. His eyes narrowed. He was going to walk out but then unclenched his jaw and nodded slowly.

'All right, tell me, why did you feel obliged to harbour an enemy?'

Hannah explained exactly how she'd become involved, that she hadn't known about Pete and Dave when she'd gone looking for the missing pilot. 'So, do you understand *now* why I did what I did?'

'I do. Thank God you weren't caught. I doubt the authorities would have seen it the same way. Look at me, darling, don't you realise whatever your motives, it no longer matters?' He gently brushed away her tears with his thumbs. 'Mind you, I might think twice if you were a dyed in the wool Nazi supporter.'

She drew back, there was still something else holding them apart. 'When you followed me, did you intend to kill Flt Lt Schumann?'

He didn't flinch from her direct gaze. 'I don't know. I was mad with grief for Pete and Dave, but also because of your betrayal. I wouldn't have fired if he hadn't pointed his gun at me. I'm a good shot, if I'd wanted him dead the bullet would have gone straight through his heart.'

This wasn't the answer she'd been expecting. 'But you thought he was dead didn't you? I certainly did.'

'I didn't care either way; knowing my actions had destroyed everything between us was what mattered. My next priority was protecting you from discovery.' He ruffled her hair. 'I don't think I told you, as far as the constabulary are concerned we're engaged to be married.'

'I was going to mention that. I called you my fiancé when

I left the letter at the base. Betty congratulated me, it's all over the village. What do you think we should do?'

His chair scraped back, the noise loud on the flagged kitchen floor. Before she could stop him he dropped to one knee and took her hands in his. He was smiling but his eyes were sincere. 'Will you marry me, my love? We haven't been together long but I know you feel the same way. There's a war on, God knows what's around the corner. Why should we waste time when we might have little left?'

It was madness to agree to marry him after exactly two weeks. 'I will. I love you.' She grinned. 'If we can still say that after all we've been through these past few days I'm sure we're meant to be together.'

His shout of triumph sent Sooty back through the scullery window like a rocket. Joan burst in her face anxious. 'Whatever's the matter? I just dropped half a bucket of coal; you gave me a real scare.'

Jack was on his feet, his smile couldn't be wider. 'You can be the first to congratulate us. Joan, Hannah has agreed to marry me.'

Joan winked at her. 'What did I say about bottom drawers this afternoon, ducks? Are you coming in to the bar so we can celebrate?'

'I want to go and see how Betty is and tell all three of them the good news. You go in, Jack, I'll be there in a bit.'

His kiss was hard, passionate, quite different from the others. Would he want her to go to bed with him now they were engaged? She wasn't sure she was ready for that. The thought of doing the same things Ralph had done made her feel sick. She couldn't help her involuntary recoil and instantly he stepped away.

'Don't look so stricken, darling, I know how you feel; I told you before, I'm happy to wait until you're ready. Being engaged doesn't change that but it does mean we can be alone without Joan getting agitated.'

His jacket was rough against her cheek and his familiar smell filled her nostrils. She loved him so much, wanted to tell him she was ready to make love with him but it would be a lie. 'I'm sorry, I love to be close to you, to have your arms around me, but … well, I can't go any further. I'm sure I'll feel differently in a while.'

'We'll take it slowly. But I'd like to get married immediately. Our squadron's being sent overseas in the New Year, I might not be back for years.'

She clung to his jacket; when he'd said they didn't have much time she hadn't realised he was talking literally. 'That's only a few weeks. Will we have to get a special licence?'

He shook his head, ignoring her question. 'I can't believe you've just agreed to marry me this year. I thought I'd have to do a lot of persuading. The padre can conduct the service, he's already done it several times in the local church. The vicar can call the banns next Sunday; that means we can be married at the end of the month.'

His excitement swept her along - nothing else mattered. They would be married and she'd be safe for the rest of her life. Ralph Mayhew wouldn't be able to touch her again. She stiffened and struggled to be free. 'I can't marry you before January 6th, I need my father's permission until then.'

His hands were firm on her arms. He shook her gently. 'Then we'll go and get it. I'll borrow a jalopy and we'll go as soon as I can get a pass.'

Despair and disappointment made her snap at him. 'Don't be stupid, why do you think I'm living here? I never want to see any of them again. I don't want them to know where I am. You must promise me you won't attempt to see him.'

'I suppose I must, if that's what you want. As you're so close to your majority maybe the padre will turn a blind eye. Are you sure that's the only reason you're hesitating?'

The rush of relief made her head spin. She opened her

mouth and kissed *him* for the first time. A clatter of feet coming down the stairs forced them apart.

'Blimey, I didn't think you had it in you, Hannah. Thought you were a good girl.'

'Jack and I have just got engaged. I was coming up to see how Betty is and to invite you both to come and have a drink with us.'

Daphne rushed forward and threw her arms around her neck. 'Betty's fast asleep. Don't worry about her. I can't believe it, engaged after two weeks and to the most handsome man in Debfield.'

Ruby added her congratulations and insisted on kissing Jack. Hannah smiled as she watched him squirm. 'Joan's telling everyone, they'll be waiting to drink a toast to us. We still haven't sorted out where you're going to sleep, Jack.'

'There are empty rooms upstairs, we can find the linen and make one of them up later. I wonder if Joan's got any bubbly?'

His question caused great hilarity. Hannah, holding his hand, led them in to the crowded bar. Their appearance was greeted by a raucous cheer. Complete strangers wanted to kiss her on the cheek and Jack had his hand pumped and his back slapped by everyone.

'Here, ducks, I think you should have something a bit stronger than shandy tonight. I've got you a nice gin and tonic; just the ticket in my opinion.' Joan pressed the glass in to Hannah's hand.

She sniffed the glass suspiciously, it smelt of tonic water and she liked that. Jack returned and slipped a possessive arm round her, in his other hand he had a brimming pint.

She didn't like being the centre of attention, but tonight with him beside her it seemed acceptable.

He shouted for quiet. 'Shut up, you rowdy lot. Now, everyone raise your glass to the most beautiful girl in the world, my Hannah, who's agreed to marry me.'

'Can't think why, mate, not when she's got me available,' one wag called out.

Another joined in. 'Beauty and the beast, and we know which one is which, don't we?'

Everything was good-humoured but she was uncomfortable surrounded by grinning faces. She gulped down her drink, it tasted innocuous enough and she didn't refuse when someone put a refill in her hand.

The pianist was amongst the crowd and soon everyone was singing. Hannah didn't know the words but was able to join in with *Bless 'em All* as lustily as the rest. Eventually the bar emptied. Daphne and Ruby promised to bring fresh clothes for Betty when they came for lunch the next day.

The bar was a shambles; Joan's friends had gone home long since. For some reason her feet seemed unwilling to go in the direction she wanted, she must be more tired than she realised. She stumbled in to a chair and almost lost her balance.

*

Jack's head whipped round when a chair scraped across the boards. Hannah shouldn't have had that last G&T. She wasn't used to alcohol. Joan had abandoned the bar, leaving him to lock up and turn out the oil lamps. That would have to wait until Hannah was safely upstairs. She stared blearily at him. 'Sweetheart, you've had too much to drink. You're more than a bit tiddly. Come along, I'll carry you up to bed.'

Her eyes closed and she sighed heavily as he carried her through to the private quarters. Climbing the narrow staircase was a nightmare, twice he cracked her elbow on the wall but she didn't protest. Good thing his shoulder was all but better.

The fire was glowing in the hearth. She'd come to no harm on top of the bed until he returned to sort her out.

Carefully positioning her on her side in case she was sick, he hurried down to the bar and completed the things Joan had asked him to do.

He checked the range was banked and the back door bolted before heading upstairs. He was damned if he knew where he was going to sleep, he'd no idea where sheets and things were kept. All the other rooms would be freezing. He'd spent one night undetected in Hannah's room so he might as well do it again. After all they were going to get married at the end of the month.

Slipping off her shoes was one thing, but could he trust himself to remove anything else? He ached to make love to her, she was so lovely lying there with her glorious brown hair escaping from its chignon and her frock rucked up around her knees exposing her long, slender legs.

She wouldn't want to sleep in her best dress and she didn't have another pair of stockings. He knelt beside her and ran his hands up her leg until his fingers touched the fastenings of her suspender belt. It was torture unbuttoning and rolling them down one by one - he wasn't sure he could take off her dress and remain sane.

Trying to think of unpleasant things and fill his head with images of battle and death helped a bit. She raised and lowered her arms obediently like a child, he pushed himself upright and flung her dress over a chair. Now all she had on was her silky petticoat.

He would have managed if she hadn't opened her eyes and smiled at him, holding out her right hand. 'It's cold without you, come in and keep me warm.' Slowly she wriggled upwards, her slip caught under her bottom and he couldn't take his eyes away. When she reached the pillow she flicked back the sheets and slithered between them. His control was almost gone.

He hadn't intended to undress but he couldn't get in with his clothes on. He kicked off his shoes, his jacket and trousers followed, then his shirt and tie; lastly he pulled off his socks. There was something about a man going to bed with his socks on that appalled him.

He was shaking, his heart so loud he thought she might hear it. Carefully lowering himself to the edge of the bed he slid in beside her, praying he could keep his passion banked down, would be able to hold her without attempting to make love.

She came trustingly in to his arms, settled herself with her head resting on his good shoulder and was instantly asleep. The pins from her hair stuck painfully in to his face; he'd have to remove them if he was to have any shut-eye. He'd forgotten to douse the oil lamp so it should be simple enough to take them out.

He removed the pins one by one; as each lock of hair tumbled around her shoulders his hold became more fragile. The pins went the same way as his clothes. He couldn't resist running his hands through her hair; he'd never seen it loose before. Hadn't realised how long it was, how smooth and silky between his fingers, how sweet it smelt as he pressed his face in to it.

'That's better, it was pulling, thank you.' Her fingers traced a pattern through the hair on his chest. 'Goodness, you've taken your shirt off. How lovely. Goodnight, my love.'

Her rhythmic breathing told him she was deeply asleep. He didn't expect to join her—holding her semi-naked body against his was going to be as much a torture as a pleasure. To his surprise he gradually relaxed and drifted off, his head full of plans for the future when this amazing girl would be his wife and one day, very soon she would also be his lover.

*

Hannah woke up. For some reason she couldn't move, something heavy was trapping her under the blankets. There was a horrible thumping behind her eyes and her insides seemed to have a life of their own. She was going to be sick.

Her eyes flew open to meet the sleepy blue of Jack's staring back at her. 'Get out of the way, quickly.'

'Hang on, I'll get the pot.' He rolled out of bed in one fluid movement and reached under the bed not a moment too soon. He held her hair back whilst she retched and removed the stinking pot when she'd finished.

'There, you'll feel a lot better now.' He tipped some water from the jug in to a glass, dipped her flannel in to the basin and handed them to her. 'Wipe your face and rinse your mouth out, that should do the trick.'

She did as he suggested, once the foul taste was gone she felt much better. Her eyebrows disappeared under her hair. What was he doing with no clothes on in her bed? Her memory of last night was blurry. Had she invited him in? 'I think I need to go outside, I'll have to get dressed, Betty has my dressing gown and I can't go out in my underwear.'

'Sit still, I'll get you something to put on.' Without a by your leave he started rummaging through her chest of drawers. Triumphantly he turned with a clean blouse and cardigan. 'Do you have a pair of slacks in the wardrobe?'

'I do, and I shall need socks as well.' Now her head was clearer she was able to see he was wearing just his underpants. She'd never seen a man with so little on, no, that wasn't quite true. She and Giles had often swum in the lake. But this hadn't prepared her for the excitement of seeing the naked shoulders, firm buttocks and thickly muscled thighs of the man she was in love with.

He turned, her spare slacks over his arm and a pair of neatly rolled socks in his other hand. She couldn't take her eyes off his upper body, she vaguely remembered touching the hair on his chest, but nothing had prepared her for the sight of blonde curls that tapered down to his waist. He was so beautiful. The strange languor that rippled through her made everything seem different. Her eyes widened as something extraordinary happened.

Was she having that effect on him? Her pulse raced, heat pooled between her legs and she shifted uncomfortably not sure what was wrong with her.

She raised her eyes, he was rigid, flags of colour across his cheek bones, his eyes almost black. He was waiting for her to signal. She swallowed. Her mouth was dry. She wanted him to touch her, to love her, to show her that what happened between a man and woman could be wonderful.

Her hand slowly uncurled, she watched it lift until it was pointing towards him. She couldn't say the words, didn't know how to, but he understood her gesture and closed the distance between them in one stride.

'Are you sure, darling? I want you so much but if you're not ready I shall understand.'

His skin was burning. He needed her, this was something she could give him, something that would show how much she loved him whatever the cost to herself.

*

Jack looked down, his eyes anxious, his weight supported on his elbows. 'Was that all right for you?'

It certainly was. 'I didn't know anything could be so wonderful. After what happened before I've dreaded doing this with anybody.' Her hands encircled his neck pulling him back down. 'It was glorious, like being someone else entirely. The only thing is - it was over too quickly.'

He nibbled her ear, his hot breath sent waves of excitement from her toes to her face. His skin was sweat slicked, her fingers glided smoothly across the contours of his shoulders, passed over his scar. His muscles moved beneath her touch.

'For God's sake, my darling, don't. Someone could come

in, it'll be light soon and Joan will be up early because of the mess downstairs.'

'We've got plenty of time, it doesn't take long to make love, we can get up immediately after we've finished.'

His lips transferred to her mouth and his tongue darted in and out, she arched towards him wanting him to do the same inside her. Her legs wound around his hips as he plunged to the rhythm of his tongue. For the second time her world exploded in ecstasy, he joined her in release and they flopped back exhausted and completely satisfied.

When he'd recovered his breath he whispered in her ear. 'It's a good thing we're getting married at the end of the month you could be pregnant.'

Intrigued, she moved away a few inches in order to see his face. 'What? If it's as easy as that why aren't all married women permanently having a baby?'

His chest vibrated, his chuckle tickled her neck. 'Probably because they don't make love very often. Also, you can get prophylactics from the chemist which prevent conception. I'll see about getting one from the doc when I get back to base today.'

The idea that Dr Donnelly would then know what they were getting up to filled her with horror. She wriggled away and gave him a sudden shove, sending him catapulting out of the bed. 'Don't you dare, Flt Lt Rhodes, I'll never speak to again if you do. If you must get one of these whatever they are, go to the chemist in Saffron Walden where nobody knows you.'

He scowled at her from the floor. 'I know we have to get up, but was that really necessary? My backside will be black and blue.'

Giggling she wagged her finger at him. 'Get up and stop complaining, I should have insisted you slept on the floor anyway and not in here with me.'

As he surged upright she realised he'd discarded his

underpants; his front view was vaguely disappointing, she much preferred his back. Somehow her petticoat and knickers had vanished as well; shy, she dived under the covers. 'I'll stay here whilst you get up, I hope you falling out of bed didn't wake anyone.'

The door had closed quietly behind him before she dared to emerge. Good grief! The pot - he could have landed in it when she pushed him out. What a horrible surprise that would have been. She hung over the side and peered under the bed - the receptacle had vanished. The lovely man had taken it, he must really love her to be prepared to do that without complaint. She was jolly sure she wouldn't do the same for him.

Warmly dressed in the clothes he'd got out for her, her hair pulled back in a makeshift ponytail, she collected the oil lamp which had burned out long ago. Using her torch to guide her she scurried to the kitchen expecting to be accosted at any moment by an irate Joan or a highly amused Betty. She met no one, she wasn't sure what the time was, but it couldn't be seven yet.

The back door was open, she could hear Jack filling up the coal scuttles. She pushed her feet in to her gumboots and put on her jacket. She'd go down to the standpipe and get some water; they were going to need several bucketsful to do all the dirty glasses from last night.

'Hannah, leave that, I'll go as soon as I've done this. You get the kettle on and we can have a cup of tea before we start.'

She dropped the buckets with the clatter. 'That's kind of you. I didn't know men could be so nice. Certainly the ones I've met weren't like you.'

He chivvied her inside. 'Go on, don't hang about out here. I bet you've got a thumping headache still. Your first hangover and it serves you right.'

Sticking her tongue out she grinned. 'Actually, Mr Know-it-all, I feel absolutely splendid. Do you think we've invented a hangover cure?'

Chapter Nineteen

When Joan appeared breakfast was ready, the bars both cleaned and swept, only the glasses left to wash and dry. 'I was about to bring you up a cup of tea, Joan. We've almost done here, and I'm doing mushrooms on toast for breakfast. Did you look in on Betty?'

'I did, she's coming down in her night things, I didn't rinse out her clothes and hang them up last night or they would have been dry by now.'

'Ruby's bringing her something to put on; as long as she's not caught pneumonia or anything. We don't mind her sitting around in your nightie and my dressing gown.'

Breakfast was a lively meal; Jack couldn't stop smiling and every time he looked at her, her heart skipped a beat. She was sure that the others guessed they'd made love but if they did they were too polite to comment.

Although Betty couldn't go outside she was happy to wash and dry glasses all morning whilst Jack and Hannah got on with preparing the roast. Over the meal Joan, who had missed church for the first time in years, offered to do their reception in the bar when they got married.

'That's kind of you, Joan. That would be perfect wouldn't it, Jack? Can I come this afternoon when you speak to the padre? Are civilians allowed on the base?'

'We've got dozens of them working up there; nobody will notice an extra one. And you're right; it'll be easier to explain if you're there.'

'What problem?' Joan asked

'I'm not twenty-one until January and I don't want to have to ask my father for permission. We're hoping we can fudge the necessary forms as it's only two months until my birthday. We don't want to wait because Jack's going to be posted overseas.'

'We're going to ask the padre on the base to marry us – he might be prepared to overlook the lack of parental consent,' Jack said.

'Hardly think it matters - there's a war on, too many other things to worry about than that.' Joan cut herself a second slice of apple pie and added a generous dollop of the thick cream. Mrs B. had sent. 'If all of us save our coupons, I reckon I can put on a good spread. It'll have to be a cardboard wedding cake but I could put a nice jam sponge underneath.'

'Never mind the cake. What on earth am I going to wear? I've got loads of lovely dresses but I left them all behind when I ran away. I'll have to go in to town tomorrow and see if I can find something. Would you come with me, Joan?'

'It would be an honour, ducks. Maybe we can find a pretty length of material; I could run you up a nice two-piece if you like.'

'I hope you're going to ask us to be your bridesmaids, Hannah.'

She beamed at her friends. 'Of course, and I'll ask Mrs Boothroyd to come as well. Do I have to ask him? He'll put a dampener on the process.'

'Someone's coming to collect me in fifteen minutes, are you ready, Hannah?' Jack said.

'I hate to leave you with the washing-up, Joan, but I'll make it up to you tomorrow.'

'Go along with you, you've done more than enough.

Get this date sorted out; I can't wait. There's nothing like a wedding to cheer everybody up.'

'I hope Jack can persuade the padre otherwise I'll have no option but to contact my father.'

*

It was a bit of a squash in the front seat of the old jeep but the back was full of some sort of radio equipment. The driver, a jolly man in his thirties, clattered the gears and put his foot down. Hannah, who was sandwiched between them, had nothing solid to cling on to. Pressing herself against the seat she grabbed Jack's arm and closed her eyes.

The vehicle miraculously slowed, the sick making jolting stopped. 'Open your eyes, sweetheart, it's quite safe.'

'Goodness, do you always drive like this?'

'Sorry, miss, forgot there was a lady aboard. The blokes don't mind, they don't like to hang about you know.'

The three miles from the village to the base was accomplished in record time. She thought they'd have to stop at the gate for her to sign something or other, but Jack just waved and they roared through. She was glad to get out, if it was a choice of returning with this driver, or walking, she'd definitely prefer the latter.

'The padre will be in his office, he's got a room in the married quarters. Do you mind if we go back to my rooms first? I want to dump my overnight bag.'

'I'd like to see them, I want to know everything about you.'

He took her hand and they were strolling through the huge camp to the officers' quarters when the siren went off.

'Bloody hell, that's all we need. The shelters are over there, we'd better run for it.' He gripped her elbow and all but dragged her along beside him. They joined a crowd of like-minded people, she hoped the shelter would be large enough to hold them all.

They dived in just as the first bombs fell around them. She'd read about the dreadful bombing in London and other cities but had no idea how terrifying it was until now. The two men who'd come in behind them slammed the door, Jack put his arm around her and gathered her close.

'God, you're shaking like a leaf. It's all right, we're safe in here. Even a direct hit wouldn't be a problem.'

'I didn't think they came in daylight and especially not on Sundays.' The shelter shook and brick dust puffed out of the ceiling. She held back her moan of fear, burying her face in his jacket instead. There was no room to sit down, if he hadn't been supporting her her legs might have given way.

'I hope the bastards don't get my new plane, I've not taken her out on a sortie yet.' Jack's muttered comment steadied her. No one else was panicking, she needed to pull herself together and not embarrass him.

'Does this happen often?' She was pleased her voice sounded normal.

'Not too often, thank God. We've had the occasional night raid over the past few months. I don't think this is a real raid, just a tip and run. Listen, the all clear's going.'

They streamed out in to the afternoon sunlight to find smoke pouring from the officers' married quarters where she could have been living in a few weeks' time. The sound of fire bells and the shouts of officers organising their men echoed around the camp.

'We'd better stay where we are until we know what's what. I think that's put the kibosh on seeing the padre, it'll be chaos over there for a bit.'

'I hope no one was hurt; there's more smoke on the edge of the camp but I can't see any of your precious 'planes on fire.'

His arms tightened around her waist. 'Hang on, here's the Wing Co, he'll know what's happened.'

Most of the people who'd sheltered had dispersed, this was all in a day's work to them, only she had knees like jelly. 'Ah, Jack , this must be your fiancée. Good to meet you, Gerald Stanton.'

Hannah took his hand and he shook it vigorously. 'I hope nobody was injured in the raid. Has there been much damage Wing Commander?'

'The bugger dropped six bombs, four on the perimeter - they've just left a few holes. We can soon fill those in. Unfortunately the damage in the married quarters is worse; the WAAFs billeted there will have to find somewhere else. As far as I know nobody was hurt.'

He saluted sloppily and strolled off. Everyone was very relaxed here, not at all how she'd expected this establishment to be. 'Are all the officers like him?'

Jack raised an eyebrow. 'What's wrong with the Wing Co? He's a great bloke.'

'I liked him, that he's … well, you know, not very military is he?'

His shout of laughter turned several heads. 'Good God, the RAF's not like the army, jumping to attention every five minutes. Let's go to the mess, you can get a decent cup of coffee there, courtesy of the Eagles.'

'Eagles? Who are they?'

'Our American brethren; they're chaps who volunteered to fight the Germans. About time their government made it official, sending equipment and things is just not enough now.'

The interior was much nicer than the unprepossessing, concrete, flat roofed building had led her to expect, and he was right, the coffee was delicious. He also came back with a large slab of chocolate, a real treat as the small bars of Cadbury's ration chocolate were in very short supply.

'An engagement gift, I wish I had a ring to give you. Perhaps we can go in to town next week and find something.'

'Actually, I'd rather have the chocolate. When do you think you'll be able to speak to the padre and get a date arranged?'

'ASAP. You know, I haven't got your personal details. I'm going to need them for the marriage licence.'

She scribbled down her date of birth, her full name and the name of her next of kin, which was her father.

He scanned the paper, almost choking on his coffee. 'Hannah Elizabeth Mary Austen-Bagshot! What a mouthful, I'm just plain Jack Rhodes.' His expression changed when he read to the bottom. 'I didn't realise you were a member of the aristocracy. Are you sure you want to marry a commoner like me?'

'He's not really an aristocrat, only a baron, a 'Sir' isn't anything special.'

'Has the title been in the family long?'

'I don't really know, I think from the beginning of the last century, but I'm not sure. The family money came from trade, real aristocrats didn't dabble in such things.'

He grinned and wiped his brow theatrically. 'Phew! That's a relief, for a moment I was worried there.'

She half smiled, not sure if he was just covering up his real feelings. 'Giles and I were never happy at home. Our mother died in childbirth, father never forgave us for taking the woman he loved. We were raised by the family nanny, a horrible woman; Giles was lucky, he went to prep school when he was seven. I had to wait until I was nine to get away. My father married again when I was ten, and I have two half-sisters and a brother.'

'I've got two older sisters but we're not close. My mother died when I was five, Dad did his best but I had a rather ramshackle childhood. If he hadn't been for the village schoolteacher recognizing I was bright, I wouldn't have gone to the grammar school. I matriculated but could never have afforded to go to university, then when this lot was in the offing I volunteered.'

After a second cup of coffee it was beginning to get dark. 'I need to find you a lift, sweetheart. Wait here, I can probably borrow a car from someone.'

The return journey was far less fraught. The little MG was faster but Jack drove with more respect for her digestion. 'I can't come in, darling, but I'll be over to see you tomorrow if I can borrow the car again.'

'Ride your bicycle, you don't need a car. Make sure you speak to the padre when you get back; if he won't agree we need to know immediately. Don't forget Joan and I are going to town to see if we can find anything for me to wear so we won't be here during the day.'

He cupped her face and kissed her passionately. 'I might see you in town; remember I've got to go to the chemist.'

Her cheeks flamed. 'Isn't getting one of those things a bit like shutting the stable door after the horse has bolted?'

'Would you mind if you were carrying my child?'

She gazed in to his eyes then returned his kiss. It was too uncomfortable to do more in the cramped confines of the little sports car. 'I should be thrilled, as long as we can get married before anyone else knows. But, if I'm honest, I would much prefer to wait until the end of the war so I can do my bit whilst you're away.'

'I was thinking, darling, why don't you marry in your land girl outfit?'

'What a horrible thought, especially the pork pie hat. You're lucky, you can wear your uniform and know you look smart.'

*

The next day Jack told her the padre refused to bend the rules. 'Don't look like that, Hannah darling, it was a long shot. We'll go and see your father and persuade him to give his permission.'

'I swore I'd never go back – but maybe with you there it'll be okay.'

'Right. I'll sort out a car and arrange for a pass ASAP.'

Joan thought going back to Bagshot Hall a good idea. 'High time you made peace with your father, love, best thing that could have happened.'

Jack told her that evening he'd borrowed a car and would be at the pub at nine o'clock the next morning. Hannah was tempted to send him on his own; she was dreading having to explain to her father why she'd run away.

She was silent on the journey apart from giving directions. The atmosphere in the car was awful; she too sick to speak and Jack looking grimmer and grimmer the nearer they got.

'Jack, this is the turning. The gatehouse is just ahead. I don't want to do this…'

'Neither do I, darling, but if we want to get married next month we have no choice.' He glanced at her and his smile gave her courage.

'You're right. Turn here.' The car swerved through the gates onto the immaculate gravelled drive. 'Golly! What's happened to the park?'

He chuckled. 'Your dad's ploughed it up to grow vegetables for the war effort. Good for him.'

He stopped the car. His jaw tightened and his hands clenched on the wheel. 'Damn it, Hannah, you didn't say you lived in a bloody great mansion.'

'I didn't think it important.'

He shook his head. 'I should have realised when I saw your father was a knight. Are you very rich?'

'I've a large trust fund which matures when I'm twenty-five or get married - whichever comes first.' Why was he looking at her as if he didn't recognise her?

The car shot forward and skidded to a halt in the turning circle. 'Do I wait here for flunkies to open the door?' His words were light but his eyes weren't laughing.

'Don't be ridiculous. All the able-bodied staff have left – only a housekeeper and a couple of ancient gardeners work here now.' She scrambled out of the car and headed for the front door. Jack could come if he wanted, but she was going to find her father.

*

Jack watched her vanish. He couldn't sit here like an idiot. He'd always known Hannah was from a different background but hadn't expected this. He followed her in to the house and hesitated in the vast entrance hall. Where should he wait?

Imposing double doors led in to a huge sitting room and he wandered over to look at the gloomy portraits hanging on the walls. His shoulders slumped. The more he saw the less he liked it.

'Who the devil are you? What are you doing in here?'

Jack swung round. Standing in the doorway was a thick-set, dark haired man. He was holding a shot gun. He tensed but didn't move. 'I'm Jack Rhodes. Hannah's fiancé?'

'The devil you are. Hannah is my fiancée. Is she here? I need to talk to her.'

'You're that bastard Mayhew. You're not going anywhere near her.'

A surge of rage engulfed Jack and he threw himself forward taking Mayhew down with him. The gun fell harmlessly to the carpet. Jack grabbed the man's collar and cracked his head on the floor. Then he raised his fist and smacked it in to his nose. A satisfying crunch and a spurt of blood told him he'd ruined Mayhew's perfect features.

The sod rallied and landed a punishing blow to his head and a second to his injured shoulder. Jack was dazed. This wasn't going to plan. Mayhew hit him again and staggered to his feet. The ominous clunk of a shotgun being loaded filled the room

*

Hannah dashed through the house to the kitchen where the housekeeper was making pastry. 'Mrs Culley, do you know where my father is? And where are the children and my stepmother?'

'Good heavens, Miss Hannah. What a surprise! Sir Andrew is in the stables I believe. Lady Austen-Bagshot and the little ones have gone to stay with their grandmother. It's so lovely to see. Will you be staying for lunch?'

'I expect so, my fiancé is here with me.' She hurtled through the boot room and in to the cobbled yard. The stables were through the archway at the back. She burst through and came face-to-face with her father. She almost didn't recognise him. He looked ten years older and his hair was grey. His expression of joy was also a shock.

'Hannah, my darling daughter, I never thought I'd see you here again. Where have you been? Why did you run away? I have been out of my mind with worry.' He opened his arms and she tumbled in to his embrace.

'I should have told you. All I wanted to do was get away from him. I didn't think you'd believe me.'

He gently pushed her away but his hands remained on her shoulders. 'You're not making any sense, my dear. What are you talking about?'

She gulped and somehow told him everything. 'My God! Mayhew's in the house. We've been shooting. I'll deal with him.'

'Father, my fiancé, Jack Rhodes is with me and he knows what Mayhew did.'

Her father grabbed his discarded shot gun, rammed two

cartridges down the barrels and raced off. Hannah prayed he wouldn't be too late.

The loud report of a gun was closely followed by a piercing scream then a bellow of pain and several thuds. Her father ran through the kitchen his face white with fury, Hannah was close behind. He erupted in to the entrance hall as Mayhew staggered out clutching his stomach and with blood dripping down his face.

Jack emerged. He was terrifying. 'Get out of here you bastard. If I ever see you within a mile of Hannah I'll finish the job.'

'Well done, young man. I'll make sure Mayhew's blacklisted. He'll not dare show his face anywhere by the time I've finished.'

Hannah flung herself in to Jack's waiting arms. 'We heard the gun and I thought he'd shot you.'

He pulled her close. His heart was thundering; he wasn't as calm as he looked. 'I wanted to break his neck but settled for giving him a good hiding. He tried to shoot me but I disarmed him. Surprised he's not in the forces—what's wrong with him?'

'He's got flat feet.' her father answered. 'Now, Mrs Culley will want to serve luncheon. I hope you'll stay and eat with us, Flight Lieutenant Rhodes?'

'I'm sorry, sir, but I can't. There's an op on tonight and I have to get back.' He stepped away and half smiled. 'I'll leave you here to catch up on news, Hannah. Take care.' Without another word he turned and strode out of the house.

Chapter Twenty

Hannah heard the car drive away. Why had Jack gone? She turned to her father who was watching her anxiously. 'I can't stay here without him, I love him and I'm going to marry him at the end of the month.'

'You heard what he said, my dear, he's a serving officer and can't hang about socialising. Don't worry, you can telephone him this evening. We've got a lot to talk about; surely you can spare a couple of days?'

She frowned. There was something wrong—there had to be more to this.

'Don't look so stricken, my dear, I'm sure he'll ring when he gets back.'

'I suppose so, but I wish he'd not left so abruptly. I'm not going to worry about it now, I'm going have a bath and get changed.'

How strange to be back in her old room and absolute bliss to wallow in a bath with double the regulation five inches. She wrapped herself in her dressing gown and padded back to her bedroom. She took the first items to hand from her wardrobe then delved in her dresser for underwear.

Her lips twitched when she saw herself in the mirror. Her plum coloured cashmere twin set was perfect but the royal blue slacks and the bright red socks clashed horribly. Too bad, as long as she was warm she didn't care.

Father was in the breakfast room where a tureen of leek and potato soup steamed on the sideboard accompanied by freshly baked bread, game pie and chutney and an apple crumble.

'You should have started without me, Father, I'm sorry I've been so long. Shall I serve your soup?' She took the place opposite him sniffing appreciatively.

'Before you start, my dear, I've got some wonderful news for you. Giles is not dead; he's in a prisoner of war camp in Germany. I'm afraid he'll be there for the duration of hostilities but at least we know he's safe and can send him parcels of food through the Red Cross.'

Her cutlery clattered to the table and she rushed round to his side. His arms closed around her and they cried together.

'There, there, my dear. I shouldn't have sprung it on you. I've known for months and I was desperate to tell you but didn't know where you were.'

She swallowed her tears. 'It doesn't matter; I always knew Giles was alive. He's my twin, my soul mate. I'll pray the war's over soon or he manages to escape and find his way back to us.'

'Finish your meal and then you can tell me what you've been doing these past months. You've been in the wars, my dear, how did you break your arm?'

He was amused by her revelation she'd been a land-girl. 'Well, my dear, I'm glad you've found your feet. What are your plans for the future?'

'I told you earlier that I love Jack and I need your permission to marry him at the end of the month.' She hesitated not sure of his reaction. 'It would be splendid if you'd give me away but I understand if you don't want to. I expect Jack isn't your idea of an ideal husband. But I won't marry anyone else.' She didn't want to invite her stepmother but it would have been lovely to have had her brother and sisters there to see her married.

'I should hope not, he's an excellent young man, exactly what I'd choose for you. However, my dear, I think he was rather taken aback by the discovery that you're a wealthy young woman. It's up to you to square that with him.'

Her excitement faded. Then something else occurred to her, something far worse and much harder to sort out. 'Do you think he's one of those men who are too proud to marry a woman with money? If that's the case, then you can have it for the others. It means nothing to me without him.'

'You'll do no such thing, young lady. Why should you live in penury on his pitiful officer's pay when you can have a decent standard of living? It's not just you, but any children you might have, will benefit. If he really loves you he won't expect you to give it up.'

'I believe that's why he left. He was shocked when he discovered you're titled, hearing about my inheritance made it worse. Can you drive me home, Father, please? I can send a message to the base and get him to see me first thing tomorrow.'

'If you insist, my dear. It saddens me you no longer consider *this* your home. However, as long as I'm allowed to be part of your life in future, I shall be content.'

Hannah returned to her seat. 'There's plenty of space where I live, Mrs Stock, does B&B. You could always spend the night.'

'I'd like that. Don't forget to take your clothes with you this time, no point in leaving them here.'

A surge of happiness washed over her. 'I have something that will be perfect for my wedding dress. I'll be ready to leave in half an hour. Do you have enough petrol?'

'I do, but not for much longer.'

With three bulging suitcases on the rear seat of the Rolls-Royce Hannah climbed in to the passenger seat. This was the first time she'd travelled in front and definitely the first time her father had driven her.

During the long journey she told him everything she'd been doing and how she'd come to break her arm. She didn't mention her role in hiding Kurt from the authorities. That was a secret between her and Jack.

What would Joan think of her arriving in state? Hopefully it would make no difference; she couldn't bear it if Joan behaved awkwardly.

The car made excellent time and the light was just fading when they pulled up outside the pub. Another car was parked in the forecourt. She was out of the Rolls before it stopped - this was the car Jack had borrowed. He was still with Joan. She couldn't believe she was going to be able to put things straight tonight.

Leaving her father to find his own way she skidded round the corner and burst in to the kitchen. Jack was sitting, head in hands, at the table; Joan was patting his shoulder sympathetically. His head shot up at her noisy entrance.

'I love you, Jack; don't think you can get away from me so easily. Joan, I'm afraid I've invited my father to stay the night, he's somewhere outside. I've brought all my clothes with me so I expect he's trying to work out how to carry a suitcase. It's not something he's done very often.'

Jack slowly pushed himself to his feet. He looked uncertain. 'You shouldn't be here, you come from another world, I'm not good enough for you...'

'I've been telling him, Hannah love, that we're all equal in the sight of God but he's not listening.'

'You have no choice, remember, I might be carrying your child.'

A suitcase crashed to the floor behind them and the contents spilled on to the flagstones in a froth of lace. Her father stepped in. 'I do beg your pardon for my clumsy entry.' He stood, up to his knees in knickers, glaring at Jack. 'You will marry my daughter, young man if I have to drag you up the aisle myself.'

Slowly a smile of pure joy lit Jack's face. 'I can see I'm outnumbered. If you're absolutely certain, my darling, that you want to marry an ordinary bloke like me I'll be the happiest man in the world.'

Ignoring her father and Joan she lost herself in a kiss which healed the rift. When he eventually released her they were alone. In the saloon bar Joan was talking volubly to her father and to her surprise he was joining in. She'd never heard him laughing as loudly.

'I'm so happy. Even marrying you couldn't make me happier. My brother's safe, my father's back in my life and I've got something beautiful to wear when we get married. What more could anyone want?

If you enjoyed Hannah's War by
Fenella J Miller then why not read:

Barbara's War

You might also like to try Fenella J Miller's Regency
romantic adventures.

The Duke's Deception

The Duke's Challenge

To Marry a Duke

Bride for a Duke

The Duke's Reform

Bibliography

Aviation - Gordon Kinsey
Looking in to Hell - Mel Rolfe
Land Girls at the Old Rectory - Irene Grimwood
The Women's Land Army - Bob Powell & Nigel Westacott
Wingspan History of RAF at Debden - Keith Braybrooke
Bomber Boys - Palmer Bishop
How We Lived Then - Norman Longdale
Flight over the Eastern Counties since 1937 -
Terence Dalton Ltd.

I found these books invaluable in my research for
Hannah's War. My thanks to the authors.

Made in United States
North Haven, CT
26 April 2022

18595950R00124